All Books by Harper Lin

www.HarperLin.com

Opera Cake Murder

A Patisserie Mystery
Book #8

by Harper Lin

Opera Cake Murder

A Patisserie Mystery
Book #8

by Harper Lin

OPERA CAKE MURDER Copyright © 2015 by Harper Lin. All rights reserved.

ISBN-13: 978-1987859089

ISBN-10: 1987859081

Contents

Recipes

Chapter 1

Clémence Damour tugged at her turtleneck sweater dress. Although it was autumn in Paris and getting chillier every day, she was sweating her buns off.

Marcus Savin's fashion show was about to start, and she was sitting in the front row, squeezed between her friends, the socialite sisters Madeleine and Sophie Seydoux. Clémence should've known better than to wear wool. She'd been to a few of these fashion shows when she was younger, and it was always boiling hot. Nowadays, Clémence was trying to keep a low profile, but Marcus was a good friend, and his collection was even inspired by Damour's desserts. He'd made a proposition she couldn't refuse, and now Damour's cakes would be coming down the runway along with the couture dresses.

The cakes that Sebastien, their head baker, had provided for the show were not edible. They had to take into consideration the fact that rail-thin models were too weak to be carrying real cakes, especially while wearing four-inch heels. The fondant and icing were real, but the insides of the three cakes were Styrofoam. She hoped Marcus's team backstage were treating the cakes well. She'd overseen the delivery of the cakes earlier in the afternoon.

Damour rarely took custom orders unless it was for special occasions, such as for a film shoot or this fashion show. They stressed Clémence out. She worried the hardest during the delivery process, when she always feared her guys dropping the cakes.

Sebastien would kill her if they did, too. He'd spent more hours than anyone on the three prop cakes and the one real one.

Before Clémence could worry some more, the lights turned off and the first model started strutting down the catwalk.

Lithe and graceful, beautiful girls stomped down the runway in mega-high heels and pastel-colored outfits to the beat of electro-pop. Most of the time, models scowled on catwalks, but Marcus must've told them to look happy, because they all had a hint of a smile on their fresh faces.

"I need that," Madeleine said in reaction to a raspberry, knee-length dress on a pale, white-blond model.

"And that," Sophie said. "The coat."

She practically drooled over a powder-blue suede trench coat over a white silk dress worn with strappy gold heels.

"He has such good taste," Clémence remarked.

"He's the next Saint Laurent," Madeleine agreed.

Clémence had visited Marcus's atelier in the past few weeks. Marcus was always working. He had a boyfriend, but he was married to his work. If he was not in the atelier, he was either in a cafe or in his home office, sketching his next collection. The man lived and breathed fashion.

A constant stream of models, seamstresses, and assistants was always in his atelier. Marcus could usually be found nit-picking the details of his latest garb displayed on a model. He'd rip sleeves away, adjust the fabric and repin them, or just decry the design altogether if he was in one of his foul moods.

But his genius usually paid off in the end, such as in this collection. Every single look was on point, and they worked beautifully as a cohesive whole.

Magazine editors and fashion writers and bloggers were snapping away on their smartphones while professional photographers and two videographers captured the show at the end of the runway.

Then the moment Clémence had been waiting for arrived. Damour's three cakes came down the runway.

The first was a three-tier cake decorated with the lemon-and-pistachio shells of macarons. The colors matched the model's yellow skirt and light-green jacket.

The next model carried the fake orange opera cake, which picked up the orange accents on a maxi print dress.

The last cake was a Charlotte Royale cake, a Swiss roll cake. Making a fake Charlotte Royale was a breeze; the real thing would've taken much longer to perfect.

She and Sebastien had taken care that the colors of the cake were as close as possible to the sample fabrics Marcus had given them. The collaboration was an exciting and unusual project. Who knew that cake and couture would go so well together?

Clémence was excited about what was to come after the show. The photos of the runway models would hit all the major and minor media outlets. Her cakes would be all over the Internet. At the same time, Damour would be promoting the same cakes featured in the show to be sold in all their Paris locations.

Marcus Savin had also collaborated with them to create three limited-edition macarons that would be sold until the end of October. That would surely get both the designer and the patisserie chain more press as well.

Clémence's parents were happy with her marketing ideas, since they were not the usual proposals their advertising team would come up with. And Clémence, too, not only enjoyed working with her friend, she was inspired to do more for the family brand. Collaborations such as this one were fun, and she'd open her eyes for more out-of-the-box opportunities in the future.

She was a reluctant fashionista, but she'd recently come to embrace the scene. The thing was, she had classic, almost boring taste in fashion. Dressing well was different from being a stylish fashion plate. Parisians, on the whole, were pretty safe with their clothing choices, sticking to beige, navy, or black most of the time. That was why Clémence didn't see herself as a trendsetter, only someone who simply wished to look nice, and her only demand was for clothes to flatter her body.

Her friends, like the Seydoux sisters, were trendsetters. Their tastes and eye for detail were starting to rub off on her. Clémence was starting to become more interested in new styles of clothing and new designers.

What she liked about Marcus's designs was that they were wearable. They were innovative without being over the top. Even though she usually stuck with neutrals, she could see herself wearing his wool framboise-and-cream striped statement coat next spring. The colors were bold, and she should really start wearing more colors for a change.

The closing model was Gabrielle. She was a twenty-eight-year-old French supermodel who'd been modelling for more than a decade. Gap toothed with more curves than the typical runway model, she walked with a sensuality that gave Marcus's gold dress more sex appeal. She was flaxen haired with tan skin that was probably a result of a recent holiday, and together with the dress, she gave the impression that she was dripping in gold or that her body was like molten gold, as if she was a statue.

At the end of the show, Marcus came out for the applause, holding his Persian cat, Milou. He beamed and bowed. The super-tall models clamored around him. As he turned to walk away, he winked at Clémence.

After the show, the fashionistas in the audience stuck around to talk about the collection. Many were interviewed for TV sound bites.

"I'm going backstage," Clémence told her friends. "Are you coming?"

"In a few minutes," Sophie said. "We promised Fashion File and some other outlets that we'd give them a quick interview or some sound bites to help Marcus. See you in a bit."

Clémence ducked and tried to escape the frenzy of the media before anyone recognized her. She was sweating like crazy, and the last thing she wanted was to be caught sweating on camera. Luckily, there were plenty of famous models and actresses to steal the spotlight, so she was able to escape unnoticed.

Backstage, Marcus was also busy giving an interview to three lucky journalists who had been able to get exclusive backstage access. The models were in a state of undress, and Marcus's team were either helping them or chatting excitedly amongst themselves, high from the success of the show.

Clémence looked around for Natalie, Marcus's assistant. Before the show, she had dealt with Natalie to arrange the delivery of the cakes. The edible cake was a surprise for Marcus. After Clémence and two of her delivery guys from Damour met outside to show her the cake, Natalie said that she would find a fridge in which to store the cake and hide it from Marcus. It was an oversized, lavish opera cake, which Clémence knew Marcus would love, and one Sebastien had taken care to make perfect.

Natalie had mentioned that she'd get it to the second floor of the building, where there was a fridge. The fashion show was taking place in the gorgeous French Archives building, and she had to wait for an employee of the building to give her the keys to the kitchen. Clémence's guys had left her to take care of it, since they had other deliveries to make, and Clémence herself had gone to sit in the front row for the fashion show.

Now that the show was over, Clémence did not know where this cake would be without Natalie. She took out her phone from her purse and tried to call her, but there was no answer.

"Have you seen Natalie?" Clémence asked a makeup artist who seemed to be waiting for someone to sit in her empty chair.

"No," the makeup artist sniffed. "Thank goodness."

Natalie had a reputation for being a bit bossy, so it wasn't surprising that she wasn't well liked by many people backstage.

Clémence decided to check in the room she knew was Marcus's makeshift office for the show. It was behind a row of screens that acted as a wall. People only went behind it to go to the restrooms.

Perhaps Natalie had gone to get the cake, Clémence thought. But there was no harm in checking the office.

She knocked on the door. "Natalie?" she called loudly over the noise of backstage. "You in there?"

There was no response. Clémence opened the door.

The first thing she saw was a knife. She recognized it. It was a special knife that Clémence had brought from Damour. It was supposed to be for Marcus to cut the cake.

Now it was stuck upright in Natalie's back. Blood drenched her yellow blouse. She wasn't moving and didn't look as if she would ever again.

Clémence screamed.

Chapter 2

Clémence stepped back from the door as the others came rushing to her from the other side of the screen in response to her scream.

"What's going on?" a burly security guard asked.

Clémence only pointed to the bloody body. He winced but tried not to react. With robotic professionalism, he spoke into his walkie-talkie, then took out his cell phone and made a call to the police.

Only a handful of the fashion set were able to peek into the room before the security guard closed it.

"*Mon dieu!*" a model exclaimed.

"*Mesdames et messieurs,*" the security guard announced in a deep, authoritative voice. "This is a crime scene. Please step back. The police are on their way."

"Who was that in there?" asked another model, a blonde who looked barely sixteen years old.

"Please step back," the first security officer repeated. "But do not leave the premises. I'm sure the police will have questions for all of you."

Ignoring the questions people were throwing her, Clémence looked around for Marcus, who was walking toward her with a questioning expression, the journalists trailing behind him.

"What in the world is going on?" Marcus asked, his cat still in his arms.

Clémence pulled him aside. "Can you give us a moment?" she asked the reporters.

Reluctantly, they stepped away and began to talk to the models and crew members, who were all in jitters.

"Can you please not say anything in front of the press?" Clémence told Marcus.

"Sure," Marcus said, "but you're scaring me. What's all the commotion?"

She closed her eyes, not sure how to break it to him. "Your assistant..."

"Natalie?"

"*Oui*. I think she's dead."

"Dead?" Marcus exclaimed.

"Not so loud." Clémence shushed him, then she sighed. "Not that they're not going to find out sooner or later anyway. Somebody stabbed her in the back. I'm so sorry."

"Who? Who stabbed her?"

"I don't know."

"Stabbed her with what?"

"With a knife. The thing is, it's a knife that I'd brought before the show to cut the cake. We were going to surprise you with an opera cake from Damour. Natalie had the cake, and I suppose the knife was around too, but somebody took the knife and stabbed her."

"Somebody literally stabbed her in the back." Marcus blinked, looking numb. "It's unbelievable."

"It doesn't look good." Clémence bit her lip. "The inspector hates me. It's a knife from Damour. Maybe it even has my DNA on it. I have to figure out who would do this before they try to pin it on me."

"Of course you wouldn't do this," Marcus said. "You hardly knew her. And Natalie, well, she actually likes you, which is more than I can say about other people."

"So she has plenty of enemies, huh?"

"Where do I begin? The thing is, Natalie can be nasty, but that's precisely why she's my assistant. She's tough on people so I don't have to be. I can be the nice guy, while she's the bad guy." He buried his face in his hands. "This is all my fault."

"Marcus, no," Clémence said. "Don't think that way. Neither of us have anything to do with this. We need to pull ourselves together and get through this."

He nodded. "The police are fools, but we can't be stupid about this, either."

"The thing is, I was the one who found her in that room. I need to figure out when was the last time she was seen alive."

"With all the chaos backstage, sometimes I even forget my own name."

"There are no cameras back here?"

"No. Not unless someone was filming with a camera phone. I don't allow cameras backstage because I don't want the models who might be half naked and getting undressed to be filmed."

"When was the last time you saw Natalie?"

He thought about it for a moment. "Before the show started. She was helping me sort out the models."

He suddenly cringed at the memory.

"What is it?" Clémence asked.

"I just remembered. I was getting stressed, and I lashed out at her because she got the lineup of the models wrong. I snapped and told her to go do something useful."

"And she did?"

"I didn't see her after that. If she was around, I didn't pay attention. I'm usually so anxious before a show that work is all I focus on."

"So she was killed anytime within a fifteen-minute window," Clémence said. "The show lasted around ten minutes, and it took me around five minutes after the show ended to get back here. That's just an estimate."

"What could have possibly happened to prompt someone to kill her in that short amount of time?"

"It doesn't sound like it was planned, since it was done with our knife," Clémence said. "But I can't be sure of that. I need to ask around."

Out of the corner of her eye, she saw supermodel Gabrielle slip out. Clémence was sure she was heading out, because she had on her Burberry trench coat on and had her oversized Hermes purse in one hand.

"Wait, where is she going?" Clémence asked the makeup artist who had been helping her.

"She's got another job lined up," the makeup artist replied.

"But doesn't she know what's going on? Didn't she hear that she's supposed to stay until the police get here?"

"She knows." She shrugged. "But she does have an appointment. The girl is always on time and professional. She's not a top model for no reason. Shoots cost thousands of dollars a minute. You can't expect her to stay behind when she doesn't know anything."

Clémence looked at the makeup artist. What she was saying made sense, in a way, but it was also ridiculous. Somebody had been murdered. Even if Gabrielle's job had been for Chanel, a modelling job was not more important than a crime scene where she could've helped by cooperating.

She knew it would be useless to lecture the makeup artist, however. The best use of her time was to question her.

"What's your name?" Clémence asked.

"Tata," she replied.

"I'm Clémence."

"I know who you are. I guess you don't know who I am."

Clémence was confused. Was she supposed to? Maybe Tata had done her makeup in the past and she had forgotten.

Suddenly it came to her when she saw the makeup scattered on the table.

Tata Milan. She was not just any makeup artist. She had her own brand of cosmetics that was pretty popular among Clémence's friends. With chin-length hair and an unspectacular face, she wasn't someone you'd notice. Her attitude was matter of fact, almost cold and clinical, but there was something agreeable in that frankness, like you trusted her to give you the facts straight without any filters.

"I'm sorry," Clémence realized. "It just dawned on me who you are. That's funny, because I just started using your concealer on my friend Sophie's recommendation."

"Sophie Seydoux? I've worked with her. Don't worry about it. How many makeup artists can you count on one hand? Most people wouldn't know what Francois Nars, for example, even looks like."

Tata must've been in her late thirties or early forties. She dressed well, in a trendy and sophisticated black silk button-down shirt printed with flamingos. She wore tiny earrings shaped like pineapples. Clémence supposed she was drawn to kitsch. She had dark features set on a olive face and small brown eyes that mascara and eyeliner couldn't enlarge. Her most interesting feature was her strong nose. Her cheeks were severe. Tata was no model, but her face had harsh angles that would've made interesting shadows in photographs.

"Did you know Natalie Albert at all?" Clémence asked.

"What do you mean 'know'?" Tata asked in her brisk way. "We know each other professionally. We don't tell each other our deepest, darkest secrets. This is maybe the second time we've met. As far as I know, she hasn't been working for Marcus for long."

Clémence had also met Natalie recently. She hadn't known Marcus that long either, only a few months, which was as long as Clémence knew Natalie as well.

"What did you think of her?" Clémence asked.

Tata shrugged nonchalantly. "I've met worse."

"Any idea why anyone would kill her?"

"Kill? I don't know. It's a petty business. I've been working in this industry for almost twenty years. The backstabbing I've seen has been brutal. Things could get heated."

"But a literal backstabbing?" Clémence asked. "Don't tell me that's commonplace in the fashion industry."

"No, but I've seen a photographer almost strangle a client to death once." Tata looked around. "When are the police getting here? I really want to go have a cigarette. Ever since they banned smoking inside, it's been hell to live."

"You need a smoke?" a model piped up. "I've got an e-cigarette."

"Oh, thanks," Tata muttered, taking the slim device from the girl's hand. "I should really buy one, although I prefer the real thing. I love the sensation of burning my insides."

Clémence bit her tongue and tried not to make any remarks. Her biggest pet peeve in the world was smoking, yet she was living in Paris, where everyone smoked. She observed the room. Everyone was talking intensely among themselves. Half of the models were sucking on e-cigarettes, too.

Tata seemed to be the only person who seemed utterly calm about the whole thing. It was as if she was used to crime scenes and hearing about people getting stabbed.

"None of this seems to faze you," Clémence observed. "You seem to be handling this a lot better than the others."

"Nobody here really cares about the death of an assistant," Tata said curtly. "They just like to savor the drama of being on a crime scene. Frankly, I'm beyond that. Other people's misfortunes bore me rather than excite me."

"You're not even curious who would do such a thing?"

"It wouldn't be surprising if any of the people here committed the crime. Like I said, this industry is full of terrible people."

Tata was saying it within earshot of the models, including the one who had lent her the e-cigarette. Clémence didn't know whether to find the makeup artist intriguing or frightening. Was she just a jaded member of a cruel business? Tata seemed to detest the very people she worked with. Clémence didn't doubt there was truth to what she said about them. There were cutthroat people in every industry, but there was an elevated shallowness and egoism that pervaded the entertainment industry, where everyone was clamoring for fame and status.

Tata had a piece of that pie, yet she didn't seem to appreciate it. In fact, it didn't seem like she had any feelings at all except for apathy. Clémence couldn't understand how she could be so desensitized to something like murder. Even though Clémence had seen more dead bodies than she could count on one hand in the past year, she would never get used to them. The fact that someone was murdered, however little she knew about them, would never cease to disturb her.

If she didn't know any better, she would think Tata was behaving like a psychopath. Did Clémence know any better?

But then again, psychopaths would know better than to express their true feelings openly, wouldn't they? They would be clever enough to disguise their disgust with humanity rather than let on about their disdain.

There were some people who were simply selfish. Perhaps Tata was right. Fashion was full of selfish people, Tata included.

The fact that somebody had been stabbed barely made a dent on someone like Tata's day. Even though Clémence couldn't understand that line of thinking, she didn't want to jump to conclusions to think that Tata had something to do with it.

But the fact still stood that Tata didn't care for people, and she didn't bat an eyelash at a murder scene. That made Clémence suspicious.

Before she could continue with her line of questioning, the person Clémence dreaded seeing came into the room.

Chapter 3

"*La heiress,*" Inspector Cyril St. Clair exclaimed, clapping his hands together. "I'm surprised to see you here."

Clémence crossed her arms and tried not to roll her eyes.

"That was sarcasm, if you didn't get that," Cyril said.

"Loud and clear." Clémence gave in; she did roll her eyes.

"So what happened here? Someone ate another one of your desserts and died?"

Clémence's face turned pink. Cyril snickered, knowing that his words had a poisonous effect on her mood. A few fashion people and the security guard were within earshot. But she would not let Cyril's words start a chain of rumors about her patisserie chain, and she pulled him aside.

"No. That's not what happened. I know you're unprofessional, but I can sue you for saying things like that."

Cyril raised an eyebrow. "Somebody's a little sensitive today."

"Shouldn't you be doing your job instead of trying to get a rise out of me?"

"*Au contraire.* I am doing my job. Whenever I come onto a murder scene, who better to go to than the source?"

He waved her to the room where Clémence had initially found Natalie.

"I hear the body's in that room," he said. "Care to look, or have you seen it already?"

"As a matter of fact, I was the one to find the body." Clémence gritted her teeth. She could hear herself getting defensive, and she had to silently tell herself to cool it.

Cyril chuckled. "Why am I not surprised, *mademoiselle*?"

It was so easy for Cyril to push her buttons. His smugness and arrogance never ceased to prompt her disdain. He was a man in his late thirties with smile lines like parentheses on the sides of his mouth. Not that he smiled. Rather, he smirked. He had a strong, hawk-like nose and green eyes that were pale, like a dead fish's.

She wondered if what she felt for Cyril was what Tata felt about most of the people she worked with.

If it was, Clémence was starting to sympathize with her more and more.

A man on Cyril's team opened the door for the inspector. Cyril put on his gloves and instructed Clémence not to touch anything. Clémence winced again at the sight of the dead body. Only a couple of hours ago, she had been talking to the dead girl.

Natalie's head was turned to the side. Her eyes were half open. With her right cheek squished on the floor, her saliva had dripped from the side of her mouth to mix with the blood. There was so much blood.

"Struck in the back with a knife," Cyril stated the obvious.

Clémence stopped herself from making a snide remark about that. She couldn't afford to irritate him, no matter how much she wanted to, since he would soon find out that the knife belonged to the Damour patisserie.

She decided to offer this fact up front, to get the accusations out of the way.

"Why did she have the knife?" Cyril turned to her with more suspicion in his eyes, as Clémence expected.

The faster she cleared her name, the faster they could move on to actually solve the case, so she helped him.

"She was holding onto it for me because we were going to surprise Marcus, the designer, with a cake."

She explained her patisserie's collaboration with the Marcus Savin collection and how Natalie had stored the cake somewhere in the building. Clémence had been trying to find her backstage so they could bring it out for Marcus.

"How do we know that you didn't have a disagreement with–" he snapped his fingers at one of his men. "What's her name?"

"Natalie Albert," the young man replied.

"Natalie here, and you stabbed her with your knife?"

Clémence sighed. "I know you'd start with that. It's not possible because I was watching the runway show. Natalie was last seen alive working backstage before the show started. There were a million cameras out there to capture me in the audience, so it would've been impossible for me to kill her from here. Once the show was over, I came backstage and asked around for her. If you interview the witnesses, you'll find many people who saw me. Marcus, for example, or Tata Milan, the makeup artist, who I talked to just before I went behind the screens to the office door and opened it. You're wasting your time if you want to pin this one on me."

"Whatever you say." Cyril shrugged.

He began to ask her a string of other useless questions, like what she had done that day and why she had come to the show. A photographer was snapping away at the crime scene, asking Cyril and Clémence to step back. The rest of the crew were noting and gathering evidence. As she spoke, she noticed a slight, faint footprint in the blood.

Clémence could see it, a very faint "S." She'd seen that footprint before. It was from a certain brand of luxury shoes, but she couldn't recall the name. It had been trendy all season, and she was sure plenty of the fashion set owned a pair of shoes from that brand.

"Look," she pointed out, stepping forward carefully, closer to the faint footprint.

"A footprint," Cyril said wearily. "We have eyes. We'll get on it."

"No, don't you see the S? It's a certain brand. Whoever killed her was wearing shoes from this brand. That's a major clue. It'll be much easier to narrow down the suspects."

Cyril squinted at the S and instructed the photographer to take more close-up photos of it.

"Well, what's the brand called?"

Clémence racked her brain. "Styra! It's pretty popular." She looked at the bloody footprint again.

"It looks like it could have come from boots, but also heels. The S is printed at the front of the sole. It's faint, but I'm sure that's the logo."

"So all we have to do is gather up the people who are wearing this brand," Cyril said. "We'll check the soles of every man and woman backstage."

Chapter 4

Clémence went home to her apartment on Avenue Kleber, utterly exhausted. She had only expected to be gone three hours at the most to support her friend at his fashion show in the early afternoon and ended up coming home at eleven in the evening.

When she opened the door, her little dog Miffy came running to her. Miffy jumped up and down, excited to see her. She was a white West Highland terrier and the happiest dog in the world. Perhaps it was the way Miffy's mouth was shaped, but Clémence thought she was always smiling. Even Miffy's eyes shone when she was happy.

"*Coucou*, girl," Clémence greeted her. "Sorry I'm late."

"I got your texts." Arthur Dubois came down the hall at the sound of her voice. "Are you okay?"

Her boyfriend gave her big hug and a passionate kiss on the lips before Clémence got a chance to reply. Arthur had recently moved in with her. They'd met because they were neighbors. Arthur's family lived in the same building, two stories down.

The two of them had not liked each other when they first met. Clémence thought Arthur was a massive playboy, which he was, but when he fell in love with Clémence, all that changed. A romantic was who he was at the core underneath the snotty, gruff exterior.

Clémence's apartment wasn't exactly hers. It belonged to her parents, who were living in Asia for the time being to oversee new Damour locations opening up in major cities. They were due back home earlier than expected, in two months, and Clémence didn't know where she would live after that.

She supposed it would be time to buy her own apartment, but would she do it with Arthur? It was time to start thinking about the future, but Arthur seemed so content in their relationship that she didn't want to have that talk with him yet. Not that she was in a major rush to get engaged. She could wait. They were head over heels in love with each other, but they hadn't even been together for a year yet. Madeleine had dated her boyfriend forever before he had proposed recently.

"Everything's fine," Clémence said. "I'm not a suspect."

"Come on, I made you dinner. You must be hungry." He took her hand and led her to the kitchen.

He had made pasta—one of the few things he knew how to make, but she beamed nonetheless. Smelling the fresh tomato sauce and cheese made her realize just how hungry she was.

"*Merci, cheri.*" She gave him a quick kiss on the cheek before sitting down and devouring the food.

"I ate without you," Arthur said. "I was starving."

"Don't worry about it. It's so late, of course you'd be starving waiting for me."

She was glad he gave her the time to eat before she could tell him what had happened in her day. Talking about it would make her ill—thinking about Natalie's body like that, the knife sticking out of her back and all the blood on the floor...

After she finished her plate, she had a glass of wine with Arthur, their preferred way of ending a meal.

"There were around forty people backstage," Clémence was saying. "A zoo. The models, Marcus and his team, a few members of the media, and me. And of course, I had to be the one to find this body."

Arthur grinned, his brown eyes laughing. "It's your fate in life."

"I wish my fate could be finding rainbows or something."

"It is. Your life is pretty great, except for the murder cases that seem to come by every few weeks."

"Yup."

"But you know you enjoy solving a good case. Who's on your suspect list this time?"

"Arthur." She looked up and smiled. "You are my Watson."

"I must be," he joked back, "since we share the same bed."

Clémence laughed and sipped her wine. Although her day had been hectic, she loved knowing that she could count on Arthur at the end of it.

She told him about the Styra footprint.

"Three women were wearing Styra shoes," Clémence said. "Gabrielle, the supermodel, left before she could talk to the police. I don't know what she was wearing. I doubt she would be the killer, though. She closed the show. After the show, she would've only had a small amount of time to kill Natalie."

"And you didn't see Gabrielle during that time?"

"No. I was still in my seat in the audience. By the time I went backstage, Gabrielle was changing, and the makeup artist was waiting to come back to help her take her makeup off. Apparently Gabrielle greatly prefers Tata Milan to touch her face, which is why Marcus paid a lot more to hire Tata."

"Who's Tata? What a strange name."

"She's a famous makeup artist. The strange name is making her millions, since it's also the name of her makeup brand."

"I know nothing about makeup," Arthur said.

Clémence smiled. "Anyway, Tata didn't seem very personable, so I don't know why Gabrielle likes her so much. Then again, I don't know Gabrielle at all."

"Talented people can get away with a lot," Arthur said.

"That's true. If you're talented and you have a lot of money and influence, I suppose people would try harder to like you. Maybe Gabrielle is cut from the same cloth. She left the crime scene even though she wasn't supposed to. Like Tata, she probably doesn't care about other people, either."

"When I was younger, I used to date models," Arthur said.

"You mean last year?" Clémence raised an eyebrow.

"Okay, okay, I know I used to have shallow taste. Until I met you. The models, well, I got tired of them looking at their reflections all the time."

"It took you long enough to stop looking at them, though."

Arthur grinned. "Men are dumb. They take a while to learn their lessons."

"I bet you had fun learning." Clémence stuck her tongue out at him.

"Let's go back to talking about the case," Arthur said lightly. "So what happened? Who were the other women wearing the shoes?"

"Let's see. Two of them were models, and one was a fashion blogger. Only the fashion savvy wear this brand. It's too cool for me. The police are probably still questioning them. They kicked me out."

"Were the models wearing the shoes during the show, too?"

"No. The models had to wear these high, strappy shoes from Marcus's collection. They're pretty cool, but not practical. I don't think I would be able to walk in them. The thing about Styra shoes is that they are relatively comfortable, because they have chunky heels. The heels are not that high, either. The models probably shouldn't have changed into their own shoes so soon after the show, since some of the press were still there, but I suppose Marcus's shoes were so uncomfortable that they had to change back. I love Marcus, but nobody wears his shoes except rich Middle Eastern princesses who never have to walk anywhere."

"So do you think the police have a handle on this from now on?"

Clémence shrugged. "Do they ever have a handle on anything? I should hope so. They have all the suspects. I hope they know what to do with them this time."

Chapter 5

Clémence's workplace, the Damour flagship patisserie, was only down the block at 2 Place du Trocadéro.

The patisserie was in a prime location with a great view of the Eiffel Tower. In the summer, patrons could sit outside and enjoy the view and people-watch, but since it was starting to get colder now, the terrace seats were nearly empty when Clémence came by in the morning.

She entered through the patisserie section to check on the selection of their baked goods. The subtle but fresh smell of the pastries hit her as soon as she opened the door, which she knew was more than enticing for the long line of customers. It was early in the morning, but locals and tourists alike needed a piece from Damour to start the day.

After greeting the patisserie employees, she crossed over to the *salon de thé* section, which was also full. Half of the tables were occupied by tourists, and the other half seated were wealthy locals who had so much money and time on their hands that they could spend half the day in a cafe reading the paper and their smartphones. Sometimes Clémence spotted celebrities in the pack, which would excite some of the staff.

She continued to the back of the patisserie, where she worked with the other bakers and chefs. Everybody greeted her with enough cheer given the time of day.

It was a big kitchen, with plenty always going on. While Clémence was an introvert who needed plenty of quiet time, she also thrived on working at Damour. She had grown up in a kitchen, and she felt comfortable and at home in one.

Sebastien Soulier perked up when he saw her.

"How was the fashion show?" he said. "Was the cake a hit? Sorry I couldn't be there."

"Oh, I guess you didn't watch the news?" Clémence said.

"No. I drove back late last night." Sebastien had been out of town to visit his grandparents in Lyon for their wedding anniversary. "And I woke up early as usual for this shift, so I'm not caught up on my Parisian news." He frowned. "Did something happen?"

Clémence sighed and told him all that had transpired the day before.

Sebastien was surprised but not shocked. Like Clémence, he was used to hearing about Damour-related murders. His girlfriend had also been falsely accused of murder once.

"It seems like there's a murder around here at least once a month," Sebastien remarked.

"At least it's not every week."

"You see the glass half full," Sebastien teased. "Only you can put a positive spin on these kinds of things."

"I know, how very un-Parisian of me. In all honesty, I still find it very disturbing. Maybe I'm just always in the wrong places at the wrong times. Hopefully the police have arrested the right person by now."

Sebastien started flattening his dough to make buttery croissants. Clémence helped him cut the dough into triangles.

"So whatever happened to the cake?" Sebastien asked.

"The cake?"

"You know, the opera cake we made for Marcus. The edible one."

"Oh, I guess with all the commotion, I forgot about it. Since Natalie was the one who put the cake away, she'd know. It's in the building somewhere, probably a cafeteria or staff room where there would be a fridge."

"So it's just going to rot there?" Sebastien sounded alarmed by the thought. "After all that work?"

"I suppose," Clémence said.

"It took a lot of work to make that cake. It's a masterpiece. We can't just let it go to waste."

An opera cake had many fine, delicate layers—almond sponge cake, coffee filling, chocolate icing. Since it was also an oversized cake, it must've taken Sebastien and a couple of helpers almost two days to make it, after some trial and error.

"That's true," Clémence said. "Maybe I should go fetch it. Give it to Marcus. Poor guy, he just wanted to throw a good fashion show. Are you free to go with me after your shift? We can take it to Marcus to cheer him up. I mean, there should be nothing wrong with the cake if it was untouched."

"Sure. You need someone to drive, right? We'll take the Damour delivery van. It should be free after the guys get back." Sebastien looked at her. "That's funny that you'd ask me to go with you and not the delivery guys. Why is that?"

"What do you mean?" Clémence said innocently.

"You know what I mean. I'm a renowned, in-demand baker. You want me to do a menial thing such as fetch a cake..."

"Hey, I'm an heiress to an international chain. I have to do grunt work all the time."

"Actually, you don't. You get our guys to deliver the cake. You could've gotten them to get it this time, too, but you want to go, and with me, too. I think I know why."

Clémence crossed her arms. "And why is that? Why don't you explain it to me?"

"You want to snoop around the crime scene some more, don't you?"

"Oh, why does everyone think I need to stick my nose into this case?"

"Because the police do a horrible job, and you love solving these things. You want me to go because you trust me."

"I also thought Marcus would like to meet the baker."

Sebastien patted her on the back. "I'm sure that's part of it, too, but admit it, you want to gather some more clues."

Clémence shook her head, then finally relented.

"Okay, fine. I guess I don't completely trust Cyril and his guys. Maybe we can talk to some of the staff at the building, too."

"Let's do it. You know, I rarely get to help you on your cases, so this should be fun."

"I think you've been watching too much *Sherlock*." Clémence chuckled. "It's not so much fun as frustrating and dangerous."

"Isn't the danger the fun part of it? It's much more exciting than making croissants."

"I thought you loved making croissants. And macarons and cakes."

"I love it, but it doesn't mean I'm always on the edge of my seat. Well, except when the milk overboils. Then I throw a fit."

Chapter 6

*T*he traffic at four in the afternoon on a Monday wasn't as bad as during rush hour. They were able to cross the Seine and down to the 6th arrondissement in less than fifteen minutes. It was September, and tourism was starting to dwindle.

Sebastien insisted on blasting eighties music through Bluetooth from his iPhone, and Clémence sang along to the Cure and the Smiths.

Paris was a pretty sight at this time of year. The leaves were turning gold and burnt orange, falling to the ground in clusters. Clémence snapped a picture of the street on her phone, particularly a grocery shop the van stopped in front of at a stoplight that she thought looked very quaint. It looked like a set from a movie from the fifties. It was so impossible to take bad pictures in Paris that it was almost unfair.

She posted the photo on Instagram. She'd started an account a couple of weeks ago to promote her art, but she found herself posting more photos of what she found interesting in daily life.

Sebastien yawned. With his early hours as a baker and the lack of sleep the night before, he was starting to feel the consequences. They parked the lavender Damour van on a side street near the building so as not to associate the brand with the crime scene, since the van had the Damour logo boldly emblazoned on both sides.

Sebastien insisted on stopping inside a cafe first, where he immediately went to a bar and ordered an espresso. It was a local cafe that was unpopular with tourists. Only Parisians over sixty seemed to be hanging around there.

A small television was hanging from one corner of the room. As Sebastien knocked back his espresso, Clémence caught the news on TV.

"Can I turn it up?" she asked a waiter.

"Sure."

The news anchor reported that police had arrested a runway model from the fashion show for stabbing Natalie Albert to death. The model was Karmen Meri, nineteen years old and from Estonia. She was a fresh face to the fashion scene. Little was known about her, but the news showed her glamorous comp card featuring the young model in strong poses wearing barely-there clothing and a bored expression.

"No news yet on why they arrested the young model," Clémence told Sebastien. "Just that they arrested her." She turned the TV back down when the news segued to a story about politics.

"So a nineteen-year-old model did it?" Sebastien asked.

"That's what they say." Clémence shook her head.

"Did you see this model at the show?"

"Yes, I think I saw her, but I didn't talk to her. There were more than a dozen other models who look just like her, so I don't think I even noticed her backstage."

Sebastien paid for the espresso, and they headed out.

"I don't think she did it," Clémence said, after they got out the door.

"Why not?"

"I just don't. My instincts say so."

"You've never been wrong, have you?"

"Oh, I've been wrong," Clémence said. "But when I think someone *didn't* commit a crime, I'm usually right."

They turned the corner. The French Archives building was so beautiful that it could've been a museum. It was classically designed, with a large garden with perfectly hedged green plants. Clémence and Sebastien needed to get past a security guard at the gate to get in, and with the events of the previous day, it looked like the security had increased.

"*Bonjour*," Clémence said politely to a humorless guard.

"Can I help you?" he asked.

She explained what they were here for, making it sound as if she was simply a dessert caterer and not an heiress who had been invited to sit in the front row of the fashion show.

The security guard took a hard look at Clémence, who was dressed down in a navy bomber jacket and dark jeans, and then at Sebastien, who still had his white baker's uniform on underneath his black parka.

"Okay," he finally said. "Go check in with my colleague as to where to go."

"*Merci, monsieur*," Clémence said brightly.

They walked across the park. Had the fashion show been in the summer, Marcus surely would've held the show in the garden. Clémence could imagine it now. They would only have to set up the seats by either side of the path, on the grass, and the models could emerge from the front door of the building.

The garden was massive. By the time they made it to the front of the building, Clémence regretted not asking at least one of Damour's delivery guys to help them with the cake. Or they should've brought a cart. She had not thought the cake delivery aspect through very well.

Two other security guards greeted them at the entrance. Clémence had to explain again what they were doing here. The security guard who looked to be in charge gave her the directions for where to find the staff break room on the second floor, where there was a fridge that possibly contained her cake.

"Do you know which of the employees were yesterday during the Marcus Savin fashion show?" Clémence took the opportunity to ask.

"Yesterday was Sunday. Most people don't come to work on Sundays."

"I know, but some employees must've had to come in, if they were to allow a whole fashion crew and their guests here."

The man shrugged. "I don't know. Wasn't working yesterday."

"I was," the other security guard piped up. He looked young enough to be a high school senior. "I don't usually work here, by the way. Usually there is little or no security here, but since there was a fashion show, I was hired. And of course, today, because, ahem, you know, the incident."

Clémence nodded. She was right about the increase in security. "So you know anyone who was working yesterday that you recognized today?"

"Yes. A redhead. She's beautiful." The man had a dreamy look on his face. "She's wearing a red business suit today and glasses. I didn't get a chance to catch her name, though."

"Maybe if you're brave enough, you'll ask for it next time," the first guard teased.

"*Merci.*" Clémence said.

Sebastien followed Clémence into the building. The place definitely had more of a work atmosphere than it had during the glamor of the fashion show the day before. Men and women in somber suits walked by with tense, pensive expressions. They didn't seem to pay attention to Clémence and Sebastien at all.

They climbed the grand marbled staircase to the second floor. Clémence found the staff room at the end of the hall. The door was closed, so she knocked.

"Come in," came a man's voice. "It's open."

She opened the door to find a middle-aged, bespectacled man eating a baguette sandwich at one of the tables.

"Sorry for disturbing your lunch," Clémence said. "We're here to pick up a cake."

"Oh." There was a slightly guilty expression on the man's face.

Sebastien went over to the fridge and opened it. He frowned. His face turned red, and he pressed his lips together.

"What is it?" Clémence looked into the fridge.

More than half the cake was already gone.

"Who ate the cake?" Clémence asked the man.

"Everybody," the man said sheepishly.

"But...it's not yours," Sebastien replied.

"I came in during a coffee break this morning, and people were already eating the cake."

"It's not right," Sebastien said. "Someone else's name is on the cake. Marcus Savin."

"Right." The man couldn't disagree with that. "They probably thought he wouldn't want it after the incident."

"So you guys just ate it? Without telling us?"

"We didn't know you would come in today," the man said. "But hey, don't blame me. It wasn't my idea."

"But you ate it, too." Sebastien fumed.

"Yeah. You can't say no to a cake."

Sebastien was about to give him a piece of his mind when Clémence cut in. "Let's all calm down."

She turned to the man. "Were you working here yesterday, *Monsieur*?"

"On a Sunday? No. Of course not."

"Do you know who was?"

"Nope."

"Do you happen to have a coworker here who has red hair and is wearing a red suit today?"

"Oh. Veronique. Sure. She's the manager of the family archives."

"Where is she?" Sebastien demanded.

"She's on the third floor. On the right wing. Her door has her name on it."

"*Merci*," Clémence said.

Sebastien threw his hands in the air as he followed her to the door. "What are we going to do?" He shot the man one last dirty look. "Marcus's assistant was murdered. Now somebody eats his cake, too?"

Clémence grabbed his arm and pulled him out the door. "Come on, Seb, let's go."

When they were back in the hall, Sebastien was still fuming. "Can you believe these people? They just assumed that the cake was for the taking."

"Oh, let's calm down. I know you worked really hard on that cake, but a cake is meant to be eaten. At least some people enjoyed it. I'm not sure Marcus would actually want to eat much of it anyhow, especially since he's always on one diet or another."

"Fine." Sebastien sighed. "I just don't think it's right. Morally."

"Stop pouting. At least we don't have to carry the cake back across the garden and down the street. We didn't even bring a cart. How dumb are we?"

"That's true. Fine. You're right."

They went up to the third floor. It took them a while to find the right door after checking all the names on them.

Clémence knocked.

"*Oui?* Come in."

Clémence opened the door. When she saw the redheaded woman, she stepped in.

Veronique was in her early forties. She was well kept in a classy tailored suit and black heels, and she reminded Clémence of a femme fatale in a film noir.

Veronique took off her oversized black-rimmed glasses and looked at Clémence and Sebastien curiously.

"May I help you?"

"We're from the Damour Patisserie," Clémence said.

"We came here to pick up our cake," Sebastien added, "but it seems like a bunch of people have already gotten to it."

Clémence nudged him in the gut to tell him to can it.

"I'm awfully sorry," Veronique said. "I was going to find out who to call to take the cake back after what happened to Natalie, but by the time I got to the kitchen this morning, some of my colleagues had already eaten the cake."

"Likely story," Sebastien muttered under his breath.

Clémence elbowed him in the ribs, harder this time. He stifled a groan.

"When was the last time you saw Natalie?" Clémence asked.

"Before the fashion show started. I was helping out, making sure that nobody was damaging anything, and then I took a seat in the audience when the show was ready to start."

"Did you help her hide the cake?"

"Yes. I helped her roll the cake on a cart into the elevator and then into the fridge. I didn't know her well, but she seemed like a smart, determined girl. I'm sorry to hear that life was cut so short."

"Did you work a lot with her yesterday?" Clémence asked.

"I mostly worked with other members of Marcus's team on the set to coordinate the space, to make sure everything was going smoothly."

"I see. Did you hear about the model's arrest?"

"Yes. I was quite shocked."

"Really? Why?"

"That model looked like the sweetest girl," Veronique said. "Why would she want to kill Natalie?"

"Why would anyone want to kill Natalie?" Clémence said. "Did you think there was anyone who didn't get along with her?"

"I don't know. She seemed...not the friendliest girl, but a hard worker."

"Why would you say that she wasn't friendly?" Sebastien probed.

"I was backstage a few times, and I could tell some of the models didn't like the way she was talking to them. Just a bit bossy and rude. I suppose Natalie didn't have the best people skills. She's quite young. Then she got yelled at by Marcus, and she was so embarrassed that she fled. At that point, I went out to watch the show."

"Who in particular seemed pleased about Natalie's embarrassment?" Clémence asked.

"Oh, I don't know." Veronique thought about it. "A few of the models. I can't speculate. I'm sure they were all quite content about that, especially after the way Natalie was talking to them."

"So Natalie's not popular with the models," Clémence mused. "They probably had to work with Natalie quite a bit, huh?"

"Yes." Veronique nodded. "I guess it is possible that a model would kill her. Some of them are so skinny. Models have a reputation of having health and drug problems. Who knows what kind of drugs they're on that would enable them to do such a thing."

Chapter 7

"What do you think?" Clémence asked Sebastien when they were outside.

"I dated a model once," Sebastien stated.

"It sounds like everyone has," Clémence muttered.

"We broke up because she travelled a lot, always flying off to Japan to work. She didn't do drugs, but she knew plenty of other models who did. Maybe there's some truth to that."

"So the arrested model, Karmen, maybe she was crazy or was on drugs or hungry or angry, or a big, messy combination of all of those things."

"I met some of my ex's model friends, too. Wouldn't put it past one of them to do something crazy. They're pretty competitive and catty. I once heard them talking about my ex behind her back."

"But even if Natalie is mean, would she be so annoying as to drive one of them to kill her?" Clémence asked. "I don't think someone like Karmen would unless there was a deeper issue at hand."

Sebastien yawned again.

Clémence smiled. "Solving crime is not as interesting as you thought, huh?"

"No, no, I'm just really sleepy. I should go home."

"Come on, let's split a cab. Maybe we should just forget about this. I mean, like I said, the police have this one. They arrested someone out of only three suspects. They can't get it wrong this time, can they?"

"Let's hope not," Sebastien said, flagging down a taxi. "I'm still really upset about the cake, by the way."

"I know you are."

"Are you going home, too?" He opened the door for her, and she got in.

"No. Even though I have to go empty-handed, I'm going to go pay Marcus a visit."

Marcus Savin's atelier was in the 2nd arrondissement. The entrance was off a little alley near Rue Saint-Honoré. From ground level, Clémence could see the mannequins and the seamstresses working through the sheer curtains.

She buzzed, and someone let her in.

Opera Cake Murder

Clémence took the narrow elevator up to the top floor, which was occupied entirely by Marcus Savin's studio.

The door was half open when she got out of the elevator, so she let herself in.

"Hello? Marcus?"

Usually there were at least a dozen people milling around, but aside from the two seamstresses working on couture dresses near the window, Marcus was alone. He stepped out from the kitchen area with a glass of whiskey on the rocks.

He greeted her with kisses on the cheeks. "Whiskey?"

His breath certainly smelled like it. He also hadn't shaved that morning, and there was not a drop of gel in his hair.

"No thanks," Clémence said. "So how are you after last night?"

"Dreadful." He was more melodramatic than usual. "Ugh. Being interrogated by the police is not something I wish upon anyone."

He waved her into the little kitchen, where they had a bit more privacy. On the way, she passed by the pencil sketches of new dresses on his work table, which was a mess. Everything in the studio was always very neat except for his table.

"I wasn't going to go in to work today," Marcus said, "but my boyfriend's out of town, and what else am I supposed to do to stay sane? I made everyone stay home—I didn't want to talk about the incident or have employees whispering, but the seamstresses had to come in to get some dresses done for a movie."

"Marcus, I'm sorry. Were you and Natalie close outside of work?"

"We didn't exactly go out for drinks after work, but even though she messed up a lot, she was a hard worker. I feel so guilty for yelling at her. That was the last thing I said to her before she died."

"Don't beat yourself up. They've arrested the culprit."

Marcus blinked. "They did?"

"Yes. I saw it on the news hours ago. Karmen Meri, one of your models."

"What? What do you mean? They think *she's* the murderer?"

"Yes."

"Are they utterly *insane*?"

"So you don't think she could've done it?"

"No way. I've worked with Karmen a couple times. She's new, very green, and the sweetest girl. When she found out she was going to be in my show, she came by with cookies during one of her fittings. Home-baked cookies. A murderer wouldn't bake cookies, would she?"

"I don't know," Clémence said. "I suppose not, but you never know. What was her relationship with Natalie like?"

"Civil, as far as I could tell."

"I do hear that some of the models didn't like Natalie."

"*Nobody* really liked her, but they listened to her. There are plenty of people in the industry who are tough, but they don't get murdered backstage."

"Hmm, right. Especially by models who are happy to be working. But what do you know about Karmen's background?"

"I know she moved to Paris just to model. She just graduated from high school—I always check because I like to hire models who are of legal age. She lives in an apartment with other models, but last I heard, she was going to move into her own apartment, since she was starting to get more high-profile jobs."

"Does she like to party at all?"

Marcus shook his head. "I don't know much about her personal life, but I doubt it. Especially recently, during Fashion Week, models work nonstop. They don't have time to party. Karmen doesn't seem like the party-girl type. She's too sweet. Like I said, she's very new. I wonder what the police could possibly have against her."

"I don't know. Maybe we'll find out soon. So you think you're going to be okay?"

Marcus held up his glass of whiskey. "Sure. It was just a huge shock. The show went so well, and then that happened. If Karmen did it, then I must be really bad at reading people. I just don't think she could do something like this. There's no reason for her to kill Natalie."

"Unless it was an accident," Clémence said.

"Driving a knife into someone's back takes force. It doesn't seem like an accident."

"True. I've heard that models often take drugs. That could drive one of them to do something crazy."

Marcus gasped. "Never my models. I hire ethically. If I ever get the sense that a model has some kind of problem—whether it's bulimia or drugs—we don't work with them. Once I even forced a model to go to rehab, and I paid for it. Having been in this industry for fifteen years now, I can spot these things a mile away."

"I believe you. I don't think that Karmen did it either."

"Then who did?"

"That's the question, isn't it?"

Chapter 8

Clémence walked Miffy in Champ de Mars early in the morning. It was grey and overcast, but the weather forecast predicted that things might turn around later in the day. The clouds, however, were threatening rain.

Miffy didn't seem to notice or care about the weather. She barked happily and took off at a run. Clémence had her on a leash and ran after her in her ballet flats.

Despite the dreary weather, she was glad to be getting a bit of fresh air and to surround herself with greenery, even if it was in the middle of a big, bustling city like Paris. She hoped the rain would stay up there in the clouds while she enjoyed the open air before she had to go in for work.

Soon, however, it did rain, and she and Miffy tried to run home before the downpour got to them. Unfortunately, by the time they went home, Clémence got soaked enough that she had to change her clothes and shoes.

After throwing on a white cashmere sweater, socks, and water-resistant black ankle boots, she grabbed a few things to put in her purse. As she passed the hallway on her way out of her bedroom, she surveyed her paintings lining the tables and the floor to dry. They sat on newspapers, and they were nearly dry. She needed to paint a couple more during the weekend to complete her dessert series.

When all the paintings were completed, she planned on hanging them in the *salon de thé*. Her friend and neighbor, Ben, who lived in a room on the top floor of the building, had suggested that she hold an art show at Damour to show them off. She could even sell them.

Clémence had always wanted to be an artist, having graduated from art school, but it was not something she'd seriously considered again until recently. She didn't think she was original or talented enough. Her subject matter was, for the time being, desserts. She wasn't exactly making grand statements with her art or doing anything provocative.

But it did take courage to do what she'd always finally wanted to do and to open herself to the public. While she hoped that people would like what she did, she would also have to deal with criticism—as she had to face sometimes in her role with the public as a patisserie heiress and sometimes socialite.

Sometimes she'd read a frivolous gossip piece on a website, then scroll through the comments. Most of them would be negative, calling her talentless or questioning why the media was even paying attention to her.

Why were they paying attention to her? She didn't really get it, either. All she knew was that she had to separate herself from the person people seemed to think she was and be the person her friends and family knew and loved.

Having had the experience of being in the spotlight, she'd developed thicker skin. It gave her the confidence to show off her art. She'd always been sensitive to critiques. Deep down, she was simply a fragile artist. There would be those who would call her talentless, resenting her for her family name and wealth, but she would deal with them as they came.

She was excited. This weekend, she was going to send out the invitations, as soon as she signed them all by hand.

"See you at lunch, *mon chou*," Clémence said to Miffy before she went out.

At Damour, she greeted the hostess of the *salon de thé* with kisses on the cheeks. Celine was one of her best friends. She'd been working at Damour for years, and Clémence had gotten to know her quite well. Celine was one of the most fun and friendly girls she knew. Her only downfall was her terrible choices in men, which included a guy she had dated recently who turned out to be a murderer. Nevertheless, Celine had been changing her dating strategy in recent days. After going on a dating detox for a month, she had gone back out on the scene to start dating again.

"How was drinks with the engineer?" Clémence asked.

"He was nice." Celine shrugged. "He's not terribly talkative, though, so I had to do most of the talking."

"Oh. Maybe he was just nervous."

"Maybe. I found the silences really awkward. I had to keep talking to keep the conversation going. Otherwise, we'd both be staring down at our glasses."

"So will you see him again?"

Celine made a face. "I don't know. Probably not."

"At least you're dating nice guys. Not bad boys who would break your heart at a moment's notice."

"I don't like the word 'nice,'" Celine said. "Why can't I just find someone who's a gentleman, but who's also interesting? Am I asking too much?"

"No. Not at all. If anything, you need to have higher standards. There will be fewer people to choose from, but you'll waste less time and energy on the wrong people."

"Well, I'll keep you posted." Celine shrugged. Her tone didn't sound so hopeful.

Clémence walked back to the store's kitchen. She could understand Celine's pessimism when it came to the dating scene. When she had been single, dating was awkward and horrible, not to mention she had still been hung up on her ex at the time. Come to think of it, she had also had terrible taste in men before she met Arthur. It was funny how someone who could seem so right for you could be so wrong and vice versa.

She hoped Arthur was the one. They had been getting to know each other slowly, but now that they were living together, it was definitely more serious. Would they really get married one day? The thought was frightening and exciting. She loved Arthur, yet she was still approaching their relationship cautiously. Sometimes she wondered if Arthur would suddenly stop loving her and leave her. It was a secret fear that she would never tell him out loud.

Trust was something that was hard for her to build, simply based on her past experiences and the love entanglements that were at the core of many of the murder cases she had helped solve.

All that was behind her now. The police were on this murder case. She had her family chain to busy herself with, and her art. Murder would not be on her mind anymore.

That was, until she made her way into the kitchen.

Carolyn, the manager of Damour, spotted her going in and went into the kitchen to get her.

"Morning, Clémence. There's someone looking for you."

"Hi, Carolyn. Who is it?"

"She's sitting in the corner."

Clémence turned to follow Carolyn's gaze.

Lowering a magazine was Lucie Harman, the fashion blogger. She had been at the Savin fashion show and had been one of the three main suspects—because she had been wearing a pair of Styra shoes.

Chapter 9

*L*ucie put down her *Marie Claire France* magazine. She stood up and introduced herself.

"Clémence, I've heard so much about you," she said. "I'm Lucie. I run a fashion website called Le Fashion."

"Right." Clémence nodded and smiled politely. "I've heard of your site."

"I saw you at the Savin show, but I didn't get a chance to introduce myself then, since it turned into such chaos near the end."

Lucie had wavy ginger hair down to her rib cage and green-grey eyes. Her black, winged liner made her eyes look more catlike. She wore a sheer white dress and patent black boots that went up to her knees. Clémence quite liked her style, and she did peruse her blog from time to time, because Lucie had her finger on the pulse of the latest trends, and she went to most of the fashion weeks.

There were fashion bloggers who were more popular, but Lucie was quickly starting to do well, and she was making her mark as an international fashion blogger from France. Her posts were in both English and French.

"*Oui*–" Clémence wondered what she was doing here, what she wanted, exactly, but she struggled to find the words to ask in a polite way.

Lucie gestured at the free seat across from her. "Can I please speak to you for a few minutes?"

"Sure." Clémence slid into the seat. She looked at her guest curiously.

"You're probably wondering what this is all about," Lucie said. "Me, ambushing you here at your work."

"Is it about Natalie's murder?" Clémence asked.

"I hope you don't mind," Lucie said. "I know the police have arrested someone, but I don't think it's the right person."

"Karmen? What do you know about this?"

"Karmen is innocent. It's as plain as day, but the police don't think to get that. As you might have heard, I was one of the suspects taken in for questioning because I wore Styra shoes. They have a footprint of someone's Styra in the blood on the floor."

"So I've heard," Clémence said.

"Luckily, the other model, Julia, and I had alibis. During the whole time that somebody killed Natalia, Julia was speaking to the people backstage, so there were plenty of witnesses to testify her innocence, and I was with my boyfriend outside, and the cameras filmed us. We didn't have backstage passes."

"I see. You're lucky."

"Yes. But Karmen is not. The police found drugs in her purse. Ecstasy. They also looked into her past, and she has relations in the Estonian mob. I don't know if it's a family member or an ex-boyfriend."

"That doesn't sound good," Clémence said.

"Tell me about it. Karmen lives with models who have drug habits. The Ecstasy could easily be one of theirs."

"How do you know?" Clémence asked.

"I'm a fashion blogger," Lucie said, as if that was obvious. "I talk to everyone and find out things."

"Are you sure the drugs are not Karmen's?"

"I doubt it. Karmen is so sweet. I'm sorry to see her reputation ruined. She's young and impressionable. I don't think they considered another suspect."

Lucie paused for dramatic effect. Clémence took the bait.

"Who?"

"Gabrielle."

Clémence frowned. She had suspected that Gabrielle had something to do with the murder, and she felt validated that someone else would think the same.

"Why would you say that?"

"She left the fashion show before the police got there. I was outside, hanging out with my boyfriend, and we saw her. I took a picture of her for my blog. At the time, I didn't know what the commotion was, and I just wanted to take a picture of her, but she noticed I took a picture and scowled at me. When I realized what had happened to Natalie, I wondered whether she was mad because I had evidence."

"Evidence of her leaving the scene? People knew she was leaving because she had another high-paying modelling job to go to. I don't think that's right, but other people seemed to think it was a perfectly acceptable excuse to leave. I figured the police would follow up with her, because I told them that she'd left."

"I don't know whether they spoke to her or not, but–" She reached into her Gucci purse, which had been hanging from the back of her chair, and took out a DSLR camera. "Look." She turned on the camera and showed Clémence the photos she had taken of Gabrielle.

The leggy supermodel had her sunglasses on, making her way to the exit.

Lucie zoomed in on her boots. "Do you recognize those boots?"

Clémence looked closely at the camel-colored boots.

"No. Are they Styra? They don't look like they're Styra." Clémence had perused the brand's website to familiarize herself with their line.

Lucie nodded. "This style is not even out yet. The designers probably sent her the boots from their new line."

"So she was definitely wearing Styras. Do the police know about this?"

"Not yet," Lucie said. "I thought I'd come to you first. After being questioned by them, I realized that they don't know the first thing about solving these things. I was talking to Madeleine Seydoux, since I was following up on doing a story on her closet, and she told me to come to you. After all, I did recall reading months ago about your involvement in helping her sister Sophie escape her kidnapping. Madeleine did say you were more astute with solving cases than the police. I figured you were the right person to contact."

Clémence didn't confirm or deny that. She didn't know if she necessarily wanted to get involved in yet another messy murder case. What was it with this city? But of course she wanted to help, especially if it meant clearing the name of an innocent person.

"I do have the advantage of getting access to the people involved."

"Right," Lucie said. "Since you're in with the fashion crowd, maybe you can find out more about Gabrielle's whereabouts. I'm just a fashion blogger. No one's taking me all that seriously. I couldn't even get backstage. Of course, I will help any way that I can."

Lucie handed Clémence her business card. It had a whimsical logo of her site, her email, and a phone number.

"Thanks." Clémence smiled.

"You have great style, by the way," Lucie said. "After this crazy mess is over, we should do a fashion story on you. That is, if you're interested."

"My style is very basic," Clémence said modestly. "That wouldn't be a very interesting post. I dress like all the other Parisian girls. It's almost like a no-style style."

"Oh, I think you're too modest. Style is about looking good and being comfortable. A lot of my readers can relate to that."

Clémence realized she should give Lucie her card as well. "Wait right here."

She went inside Carolyn's office and looked through a drawer holding some business cards. She rarely needed to give out her own business card.

Clémence went back to hand Lucie a Damour card with her name on it. "You can also contact me if you have more information."

"Sure." Lucie smiled. "And I'll contact you about the fashion story as well?"

"Okay. Why not?"

"Talk to you soon. Cute tea salon, by the way."

Lucie walked away to pay for her coffee at the cashier's counter.

Clémence went into the kitchen, her thinking space, turning the new information Lucie had given her over in her head.

The real investigation was about to begin.

Chapter 10

Gabrielle. What did Clémence know about Gabrielle? Aside from the fact that she was a supermodel engaged to a billionaire media mogul, not a whole lot.

Gabrielle was like a statue. She wasn't someone you were supposed to talk to. Backstage at the Savin show, Gabrielle had been quiet. Others, including Clémence, saw her as intimidating. Her beauty was otherworldly.

It was true that her schedule was packed. Gabrielle worked nonstop. Marcus had even mentioned that he'd been lucky to book Gabrielle to close his show. To stay on top, Gabrielle had to manage her time well. Maybe she managed it a little too well.

Clémence had noticed when she'd been backstage that Gabrielle would only schmooze with the important people: the famous designer, the famous makeup artist, and some members of the press. Was that how she had gotten to the top?

In the kitchen, Clémence got out her iPad from her purse and started to read about Gabrielle online.

She'd been born in the suburbs of Paris and was discovered by a scout when she went to a concert. She'd been eighteen, and after struggling with modelling for a year in Tokyo and other cities in Asia, she went to New York and landed a campaign with Prada. And the rest was history. Now she was twenty-eight and still on top.

What could she possibly have gained by murdering someone? Her life sounded great—traveling around the world, working only the best shows and landing million-dollar contracts. She was rich, and even if her career stalled, she wouldn't need to worry because she'd be married to a billionaire.

Karmen could still be guilty, but Clémence needed to check out Gabrielle's angle as well. She was the only other suspect. The facts that she was wearing Styra shoes and was seen coming out of the show in a hurry were suspicious.

Clémence wondered if Gabrielle still had blood on the bottoms of her boots. Had she had time to wipe any traces of evidence from her clothes and shoes? Was that why she'd been in a rush to leave? Was that why she was peeved when Lucie took her picture?

In any case, she needed to find out more about Gabrielle.

"I know that look."

Clémence looked up and saw Berenice, another baker and Sebastien's sister, staring at her curiously.

"What look?" Clémence asked.

"That look you have when you're concentrating on a case," Berenice teased. "Sebastien told me about your trip to the Archives building. You're onto something, aren't you?"

"Well, I just got new information. Gabrielle might have something to do with this."

"Gabrielle, the supermodel?" Berenice looked surprised. "I was shocked when they arrested a regular model, but a supermodel? Why?"

"I don't know. I have to call Madeleine to find out."

She excused herself and went home. There was little privacy at Damour, and whenever she was trying to solve a murder case, she couldn't think about baking anyway. She wanted to go home, take out her notebook, and try to lay out all the facts clearly on paper.

Miffy was surprised to see her back at the house so early. She was chewing on a rubber bone, but at the sight of Clémence, she dropped it and ran to her.

"Did you miss me, girl?" Clémence cooed at her adorable dog. She always thought that if she never had children, she would be just as happy with Miffy to take care of.

Miffy licked her cheek as a sign of affection.

"Come on, girl." She led the way into the kitchen, where she kept her notebook filed with some cookbooks inside an armoire.

"What do we know so far?" she wondered out loud.

She started writing all the facts she knew about Natalie, then Karmen and Gabrielle. She also included pages for Lucie and the other model, Julia.

"Plus the makeup artist," Clémence said. "Can't forget about her. Chances are she was working backstage the whole time. The curious thing about this is that everyone backstage was so busy, too busy to notice the murder, and the murder happened quickly. Does this mean that it was planned? Did someone just slip in, kill Natalie, and slip out without anyone noticing? And why at a fashion show?"

She looked down at Miffy at her feet, who only answered by wagging her tail.

"Okay, let's just say it was Gabrielle. She had just come off the runway. She changes by going to the restrooms, so no one can take a photo of a top model naked. On her way back, she is accosted by

Natalie. So Gabrielle goes into the office alone with Natalie. They argue. She finds the knife and kills her? I suppose that's plausible, in the craziest way."

Clémence sighed. Who knew what went on inside the heads of people these days? What was the motive for killing someone? Usually it was to hide something. Was it Karmen, who wanted to hide her mob connection? Or was it Gabrielle, who wanted to hide—what was it she wanted to hide? Her life was too perfect.

Clémence took her cell phone from her bag and called Madeleine.

"Âllo?" the socialite answered.

"Hey, it's Clémence."

"Clémence," Madeleine greeted her. "Did that blogger, Lucie, get in touch with you?"

"Yes. In fact, she stopped by my store today." Clémence filled her in. "Do you know Lucie well?"

"Not well, but I've met her a couple of times at fashion events. She seemed nice, and I checked out her blog. It's pretty good, and I like her style, so I agreed to do a story about my closet with her. She said she felt that Karmen's arrest was strange, so I suggested she get in touch with you. Did you guys find out something?"

"Well, we came to the conclusion that Gabrielle might be the killer."

Madeleine gasped. "Gabrielle? No way!"

"Yes. So I'm calling to see what you know about her. Are you friends with her?"

"Friends? I wouldn't say that. I'm not famous enough to be her friend. I've maybe exchanged two words with her."

"So you think she's quite frosty?"

"Maybe. Mostly, I think she's busy. She doesn't seem to have time to socialize, always running from place to place, and I also get the impression that she doesn't open up easily—trust easily, I suppose."

"But she does seem to have a lot of friends in high places."

"In high places, precisely. All the major magazines' editors, photographers, and other A-list celebrities love her."

"Why do you think that is? Is she that charming?"

"Oh, maybe. She never gives me the time of day, so I wouldn't know. When she comes into the room and sees no one worth talking to, she keeps to herself."

"Do you know anyone who *is* a good friend of hers? I want to talk to her. I would like to talk to Gabrielle directly, too, but I want to know the best way to approach this."

"We're represented by the same modelling agency," Madeleine said. "Not the same agent, but I know who her agent is."

"Really? Can you get me an appointment?"

"Sure."

Chapter 11

*C*lémence braced herself against the wind. Her scarf unraveled around her neck and threatened to fly away. She reached out and grabbed one end and looped it back twice around her neck.

The NEXX Modelling agency was in the 8th arrondissement, and as she approached the building, she went over what she would say to the agent in her head.

Somebody buzzed her in at the front door, and she pushed through the heavy red door. It led to a small garden. Following Madeleine's texted directions, she walked to the back, toward a small blue door on the right side.

She passed by a young man who was tall, pale, handsome in a feminine way, smiling for photos as someone snapped away behind a big camera. He was probably a new male model recruit with nothing in his portfolio so far. The scene amused Clémence. To see an amateur model posing nervously and awkwardly for the camera was endearing.

Clémence pushed through the door and walked up to the second floor. When she went inside to the waiting room, three young women were already sitting on the cream leather sofas, leafing through magazines or glued to their smartphones.

After Clémence sat down, two more young women came in through the door, all very young but very tall, with cheekbones that were sharper than knives.

She supposed they were here to land modelling agents. And why was Clémence here? To land a murderer.

The other girls, the ones who weren't texting like crazy, sized Clémence up. It didn't seem to take them long to realize that Clémence was no competition, and they went back to looking at their phones and magazines.

At five foot four, Clémence was not built for this industry. She also ate too many sweets to fit into sample sizes, not to mention that she was pushing thirty, the age of retirement for many models.

She checked in with the receptionist, telling her that she had an appointment with Alice Ambrosia. Some of the young girls looked up at Clémence at the sound of the name. Alice was a top agent in the industry. If a model signed with her, she was almost guaranteed major contracts.

As Clémence sat back down, the girls seemed to be glaring at her. They were probably curious why Alice Ambrosia would possibly want to see her.

One of the girls was scrutinizing her more than the others, a blonde with light-blue eyes, thin lips, and striking cheekbones, who took off her earbuds when Clémence sat opposite her.

"Hey, are you...?" She trailed off, as if trying to recall Clémence's name.

The other girls looked between the blonde and Clémence, as if wanting to say "Who? Is she someone important?"

Clémence gave no answer. Maybe the girl had seen her on a gossip blog or one fashion site or another, but she wasn't going to let on. She blinked back at her innocently, oblivious to her line of questioning.

"You look familiar," the model finally said.

"So do you," Clémence said. "You look like Claudia Schiffer."

"Who?"

"Claudia Schiffer. You know who that is?"

"No," she replied.

Clémence supposed she was too young to know who the supermodel was.

"Maybe you can Google her," she suggested lightly. It was all young people had to do nowadays to find out anything.

Clémence realized how old she felt sitting next to these young models. Although it felt like only yesterday that she had been eighteen herself and starting university, to these girls, she was probably ancient. After all, she hadn't grown up with search engines and social media. She remembered her family using encyclopedias to get information, or they had to go to the library. It was strange how much the world had advanced, technologically, in the past decade. There was no privacy anymore.

Privacy. How could a murder possibly be private at a fashion show? There were cameras everywhere. People with camera phones in the audience filmed everything. Yet five minutes backstage was all someone needed to kill Natalie. How? And why?

"Clémence?" the receptionist called. "Alice is ready to see you now."

"Clémence Damour," the model exclaimed. "Oh!"

Clémence smiled at her as she got up. The other girls were tittering amongst themselves.

She followed the receptionist's instructions to go down the hall to the last room on the right.

"Come in," Alice instructed after Clémence knocked on the door.

"*Bonjour,*" Clémence said.

Alice was in her fifties. She wore a chic burgundy skirt and a black-and-white triangle-patterned blouse. Her hair was a sleek salt-and-pepper bob that curled into her chin. She smiled with burgundy lips that matched her skirt.

"Please, sit down."

Clémence closed the door and sat down, feeling awkward all of a sudden in the office. The walls were black, but much of the furniture and decor was gold. It was definitely dramatically decorated.

She felt like a show dog about to be judged, in the same way that the flurry of paparazzi had made her feel in the summer, when she had been the target of tabloid fodder after Sophie's kidnapping.

She introduced herself, and Alice cut her off.

"I know who you are." Alice's voice was hard but her smile evened out the harshness. "You're a natural."

"I'm sorry? A natural what?"

"Model, of course. I saw you in the papers wearing the Marcus Savin dress that made all the fashion magazines."

Alice was referring to the time she had been photographed leaving the police station.

"I didn't know you were interested in modelling until now," Alice continued. "Do you have a portfolio?"

"Er, no." Clémence was confused. What exactly had Madeleine told the agent? "Did Madeleine tell you I was here about modelling?"

"Yes. Well, she said you wanted to speak to me. I naturally assumed. What did you want to speak to me about?"

"Well, I know that you are Gabrielle's agent, and I wanted to talk to you about possibly doing a project with her."

"Oh?" Alice was intrigued. "What kind of project?"

"As you may know, my family owns the Damour patisseries."

"Yes, yes, of course I know." Alice waved the information away, as if she was insulted to be told something so obvious.

"One of my new marketing ideas is to collaborate with high-profile tastemakers on new macaron flavors. I thought it would be interesting if we could collaborate with Gabrielle on developing her own macaron flavors. As you know, we've had a successful collaboration with the Marcus Savin label recently. The limited-edition macarons and cakes sold very well. We figured that our next collaboration would be with a model, since we can also shoot a series of ads to be placed on billboards and in magazines."

Alice slowly nodded, warming up to the idea. "That's not bad. It's an interesting proposition.

Gabrielle has worked with practically everyone in fashion, but a luxury patisserie chain would be the first. It's most unexpected, and she gets to put her personal stamp on a dessert...yes, I think she would really like the idea."

"Great," Clémence chirped. "Can you tell me more about Gabrielle? What her personality is like, what she does in her spare time?"

"Gabrielle is a busy woman. In fact, when she's not working, she's planning her wedding—maybe the macarons can be wedding themed?"

"That could be something to consider," Clémence said. That was, if this collaboration were actually to happen, which it wasn't. She wasn't about to work with a murderer if she could help it.

"Who are Gabrielle's friends?" Clémence asked. "Does she mostly hang out with other celebrities, or does she have, say, childhood friends?"

"I don't know about childhood friends. Actually, I don't know, now that I think about it. I don't think I've ever seen Gabrielle outside of work events. At parties, she's usually with her fiancé."

"So she's not a girl's girl?"

"I don't know. Is that important for this campaign?"

"Yes. I just want to get a better idea of who Gabrielle is. We want to sell a macaron that represents her."

"Of course," Alice said.

"Perhaps it's better if I have a chat with Gabrielle directly?"

"Her schedule is jam packed this week. She's flying back to Paris tonight after a photo shoot for Vogue in Morocco."

"This will be a huge campaign. One that we'd like to get started right away for Christmas, if Gabrielle accepts. If it's possible, I could even go on one of her shoots and just have a chat with her. I mean, models have a lot of downtime in between shoots, don't they?"

Alice thought about it. "That might be arranged. She's doing a commercial for BISOUX Cosmetics in the next two days. I'll call Gabrielle and try to arrange something."

"Thank you so much."

Alice's phone rang, and she answered it, speaking in rapid tones. Clémence figured it was time for her to leave. All she wanted to do was speak to Gabrielle. A fake collaboration had seemed the best way to do it, and it worked.

When Alice got off the phone, Clémence was gathering her things to leave.

"Clémence." Alice smiled again, her burgundy lips spreading across her pale face. "What about you?"

"What about me?"

"Are you interested in modelling?"

"I'm no model. I work at a patisserie."

"But you could be more. Our agencies sign singers, athletes, and other personalities. You don't need to be a *model* model to be in magazines. I'm sure, if you wanted to, I could land photo shoots for you, and they can even interview you about your chain. You can be the face of your company, even more so than you are now."

"Thanks. I take that as a big compliment. At the moment, I don't think I'm comfortable being the face of anything."

"Come now. You're too modest. Well, give me a call if you ever feel you're ready."

Alice passed her a business card. Girls would kill to land a contract with Alice. Clémence didn't even have a desire to be a model, and Alice wanted to sign her.

Girls would kill to land a contract with Alice. Girls would kill to be a model.

Was that why someone would kill Natalie? Had she been in someone's way?

Chapter 12

Marcus had told her that Natalie's funeral was later at seven in the evening. Clémence planned on going with him.

Natalie was often mean to the models. What if Natalie was a failed model herself and resented the successful ones? She was about Clémence's age, but she was tall enough to be a model, with the figure to match.

Maybe Natalie had had a few heated words with Gabrielle in private, and Gabrielle was angry enough to grab the nearest thing around and stab her. Gabrielle was blinded with anger and then went back to the washroom to wash off any traces of blood before sitting back in the makeup artist's chair to remove her makeup.

It was only an idea; Clémence had no proof of any of this. But what she did have was some time. Since she had to wait to hear back from Alice in regards to meeting Gabrielle, she could do more research on Natalie.

Clémence had some time to kill before Natalie's funeral. She didn't want to go back to work; whenever she was solving a murder case, she could never get into the spirit of baking. All she wanted to do was study the case until it was closed.

She decided to pay her friend Cyril a visit.

The police headquarters was at 36 quai des Orfèvres. It was still windy out, but Clémence decided to walk. She went east to Rue du Louvre, then walked down the rest of the way along the Seine.

Clémence couldn't pick out her favorite neighborhood of Paris; each arrondissement was so different with its own delights and misgivings. Her favorite place to walk had to be along the Seine. Even if sometimes tourists with cameras got in the way, the view was something she could never get tired of.

The police station was on the Cité island, near Saint Chapelle. When Clémence entered, she saw that the receptionist was preoccupied with a group of police officers. Since Clémence knew exactly where Cyril's office was, she slipped away up the staircase.

She knew she could usually find Cyril in his office. He was the type of man who would rather relax in an office than do the dirty work of being out in the field. He'd rather command from the height of a throne than perform any of the labor himself. Come to think of it, he wasn't much of a thinker, either. In Clémence's eyes, he was pretty much a village idiot who lucked out and somehow got to be a detective.

How did that happen? Clémence often wondered. Did he come from a connected family? Did he have friends in high places? It was one mystery Clémence would never solve.

His door had his name stenciled on the glass window. She knocked. Someone inside could be heard shuffling papers.

"*Oui?*" came Cyril's bored tone.

It would've been wasted effort to ask Cyril if she could come in, so Clémence simply let herself in.

"Oh," Cyril's voice deflated even more at the sight of her. "What do you want?"

The detective was tall and skinny like a beanpole, with beady green eyes and a hawk-like nose. He had his legs crossed and propped up on his desk; they were so long that they reminded her of grasshopper legs. He was in his mid-thirties and a bachelor. Clémence couldn't imagine a woman who would put up with someone so insufferable.

"I thought you'd be happy to see me," Clémence said.

"Aren't I always?" Cyril snorted.

"You should be. Especially since you know that I solve all your cases for you."

"Hardly. You solve the cases that involve products from your patisserie chain. I'm starting to wonder if it's a marketing strategy."

Clémence suppressed an eye roll. It was too easy to get sucked into an exchange of insults with Cyril.

"I didn't come here to banter," she said.

"Then why are you here?" Cyril asked, shuffling some papers in his hands to make it seem as if their contents were far more interesting than interacting with Clémence.

"I just wanted to see how you were doing with the case. I heard you arrested Karmen Meri."

"What's it to you?" Cyril sneered. "Jealous that we nailed the perp this time?"

"How do you know it's Karmen? Do you have proof?"

Cyril crossed his arms. She detected a defensive expression on his face, and she leaned back, anticipating the information that she had come to hear.

"Karmen Meri has family in the Estonian mob. They have a history of violence. She was missing at the time of the murder, and she was wearing Styra shoes."

"Where was she?" Clémence asked. "Where did she say she was at the time of the murder?"

"Some story about how she was in the bathroom, throwing up."

"Bulimia?" Clémence asked. She found that more believable than Karmen killing Natalie.

"Yes, but no one saw her in that bathroom, or going in or out of it."

"What's her connection to Natalie? Why would she want to kill her?"

"We interrogated a lot of people. A couple of girls admitted that Karmen was not a fan of Natalie, that she had even mocked her."

"What else?"

"Karen didn't like Natalie."

"That's it?" Clémence asked. "That's all you have to incriminate her for murder?"

Cyril's eyes bugged out. "What else do you need? There is no one else. Like I said, someone from a mob family must have a pretty quick temper. Perhaps Natalie said something to annoy her, and she just wanted to hurt her and stuck a knife in her."

"Karmen gave a candid interview in an article I read on my phone on the ride over here," Clémence said. "Modelling was her ticket to a better life. It was her stepfather and stepbrother who were connected with the mob, and she didn't grow up with them, nor was she ever influenced by the mob. As soon as her mother married into the mob and didn't seem to want to get out of it, Karmen was starting to get modelling work, and she moved to Paris shortly afterwards. The mob connection is not very incriminating. Everyone I've talked to said she's a sweet girl."

"It's always the sweet ones."

Clémence sighed, trying not to lose her patience with him. It was like talking to a brick wall most of the time.

"Look, this girl might be innocent, and you don't sound like you care."

"All right, who do you think is the killer? Do you have any better ideas?"

"What about Gabrielle?"

"What about her? We talked to her at length, and she didn't do it."

"How do you know that? She was also missing backstage during the time of the murder, and she was wearing Styra shoes. Plus, she went out before the police came."

"Yes, Clémence," Cyril said in a patronizing tone. "We're aware of that. Like I said, we looked into it, and she's innocent."

"Really? How?"

"Gabrielle is too...charming to be a killer."

"You're basing her innocence on charm? You know, there are psychopaths out there who are extremely charming."

"Clémence, you don't know what you're talking about. We don't have anything on Gabrielle or the blogger or the other model, whatshername. It's Karmen."

"What about Natalie?"

"What *about* Natalie?" Cyril retorted. "She's dead. She's not a suspect."

"I know that." Clémence wanted to tear out her hair. Of course Natalie wasn't a suspect in her own murder. "I mean, what do you know about her? Why would anyone want to kill her?"

"Natalie Albert...she was not very significant. She went through school an average student, didn't go to college. Modelled for a while, then worked for Savin."

"What did she model for? I didn't know she was a model." Although she had suspected it.

"She did some lingerie modelling. Catalogs, websites." Cyril smiled. "I checked out her work."

Clémence couldn't suppress an eye roll this time. "Classy, checking out a dead girl."

"It's part of my profession."

"Why did she quit?"

"Her agent dropped her."

"Why?"

"I don't know. Maybe she wasn't getting the right work."

"Who was her agent?"

"The Dexter Agency."

"Haven't heard of it," Clémence said. "It must be a smaller agency. Do you know if she really wanted to be a model?"

"She moved here from a small town to model, with no education and no other backups, so I might say so. Why? Where are you going with this information?"

Clémence brightened up. "*Merci*, Cyril. Sometimes I really don't know how you got this job, but I suppose you do do your homework once in a while."

Chapter 13

Marcus Savin was a sobbing mess at Natalie's funeral. Clémence knew Marcus was sensitive and dramatic, and with that combination, there was no stopping him from making those kinds of scenes. He was wiping his tears away with a purple silk handkerchief monogrammed with his initials, then blowing his nose into it.

There were few other people at the funeral. A few members of Marcus's fashion team, Natalie's mother, and a friend named Clarisse.

Natalie's mother's speech made Marcus cry even harder.

"...She was my little girl, and I'll always miss her. Natalie was my only child. I lost her once when she moved away, and I can't believe I'm losing her again, this time forever. Natalie was always strong willed. She grew up wanting to work in the fashion industry. Her room was plastered with magazine cut-outs of her favorite models and actresses. She had a dream. A dream to go to Paris and work in the field that made fantasy a reality on celluloid. I hope wherever she is now, she's living that dream for eternity. Thank you."

She stepped down, sobbing into a tissue. Guests consoled her, giving her their condolences.

The first person Clémence went to was Clarisse. She seemed like a shy creature, very pale and very small. She didn't look like she was from Paris, judging by her oversized black sweater and pleather shoes. Clarisse was probably Natalie's childhood friend.

"Hi," Clémence said. "It's so sad, isn't it?"

"Yes." Clarisse nodded somberly. "How did you know Natalie?"

"She worked for my friend Marcus." Clémence nodded in the direction of Marcus, who was sobbing in Natalie's mother's arms. "What about you?"

"We went to school together."

"Were you close friends?"

Clémence noticed that Clarisse's mouth twitched. "Well, we met when we were twelve, and we stayed friends for a long time until in high school. Best friends, in fact. Then we grew apart. I was more interested in books and she in fashion."

"Oh, I see." It was natural that friends would drift apart at that age. Clémence hardly spoke to her childhood friends anymore.

"So what was Natalie like?" Clémence asked. "I didn't know her well."

"She was very—" Clarisse's eyes searched above as if for the right words to appear over Clémence's head. "Passionate. I liked her because she was bold, you know? She never took crap from anybody. If anybody was mean to her or to me, she always stood her ground, even though she didn't exactly pack a lot of muscle. I would always be grateful for that, even though we weren't exactly speaking in the last two years of high school. Then she left for Paris, and this is the first time I'm seeing her since then. It's sad."

Clémence nodded. She could sympathize with the young woman. It sounded like Natalie had been one of those friends who you love but who could hurt you all the same.

"Have you heard about Karmen? The person arrested for being, well, involved in Natalie's death?"

"It's surprising," Clarisse said. "Natalie could be tough, and her aggressive personality could be off-putting to some people, but I didn't know her to be mean-spirited. Sure, she could get on some people's nerves sometimes, but I've also seen her back down and apologize when she really did hurt someone's feelings. This model must have serious problems if she killed Natalie."

"Did Natalie want to be a model at some point?"

"Well, I always knew she wanted to work in fashion. Neither of our families had a lot of money growing up, so Natalie and I used to go to second-hand clothing stores together. I just bought some necessities, but she took it to another level. She'd put together clothes in a way that was different from everybody else, and she was teased for it, but she always looked stylish. We come from a town that didn't think much about fashion and trends."

"I see."

"I don't know what she wanted to be. One minute she wanted to be a fashion designer. The next minute, a model, and the next, a stylist. I think she just wanted to be in the industry. I was quite surprised that she ended up working for a famous designer. I'm proud of her. She made it so far. Imagine how much farther she could've gone." Clarisse began to tear up. "Anyway, if you'll excuse me, I have to be catching my train home soon, after I pay respects to her mother."

"It was lovely talking to you," Clémence said.

"The same to you."

Clarisse left Clémence confused. There went her theory of Natalie being jealous of other models.

It sounded as if Natalie had been on the right track in life. She had a job with Marcus Savin. If she wanted to work in fashion, there was no better designer to work for. No wonder she no longer modelled.

But was it also why she treated models with disdain, because she didn't respect them? Did she feel superior to them once she started working for Marcus? It was a possibility. It happened in the industry, or any industry with a hierarchy.

Gabrielle was still the main suspect. But Clémence still saw no connection between her and Natalie.

Clémence waited for Marcus to finish speaking to Natalie's mother, but he seemed to be pouring his heart out.

"Clémence!"

She turned around to find Lucie, the Le Fashion blogger.

"*Bonsoir,*" Clémence said.

"I'm so sorry that I'm late," Lucie said. "Got caught up interviewing an up-and-coming fashion designer for my site, and things dragged on. I really wanted to be here for Natalie. Did I miss something?"

"A speech from Natalie's mother," Clémence said.

"It must've been an emotional speech." Lucie watched Marcus sob.

"It was."

"Well, I'm glad I caught you. How are things going?"

"Okay." Clémence supposed Lucie meant about the case. "I mean, the police still think Karmen did it. I'm sure they've scheduled the trial, but I don't know the details. I want to talk to Gabrielle, but she seems so hard to get a hold of."

"Yes, she's quite elusive, isn't she?" Lucie said. "Be careful with her. It's hard to dig up anything from her past. It's like she hasn't got one. Believe me, I tried. It's hard to be a sleuth." She let out a small laugh.

Tell me about it, Clémence thought, but she only smiled in response.

"I don't know how you do it," Lucie said. "But I'm sure you're making progress. You'll find out the truth."

"But what if Karmen did do it?" Clémence wondered. "It's either Karmen or Gabrielle. What if the police are right?"

"If you don't try, an innocent woman will be in jail. They send people to jail all the time for crimes they didn't commit. We can't let the real killer get away with it just because she's a top model and she has influence."

Clémence sighed. "You're right. I'm trying my best."

"I know you are," Lucie said. "Gabrielle is hiding something, something shameful. She killed Natalie because Natalie knew about it. That's my theory, anyway."

"Well, thanks," Clémence said.

"I better go pay my condolences," Lucie said. "Good luck."

After walking Marcus back to his apartment, Clémence went to a nearby cafe to relax. Marcus was still very saddened and wanted to be left alone. Clémence was surprised by how affected he was. Part of it must still be guilt that the last thing he'd said to Natalie had been an insult.

The cafe terrace she sat at had a view of a small park. It was chilly, but she was right next to a heating lamp. The sun was setting fast, filling the park with a wash of pink and gold. Kids were squealing as they swung on swings and balanced on teeter-totters.

Clémence rubbed her cheeks, warming them up, as she waited for her café crème. She felt like she was getting nowhere. An innocent woman like Karmen might go to jail if she didn't find out who the real culprit was.

She sat there, trying to relax, although her mind was going in a million directions, trying to piece the moment of the crime together and imagining all possible scenarios with the people involved.

Natalie was still turning out to be a bit of a mystery. She had hardly anybody in her life, based on what she could tell from the funeral. Only a mother who Natalie had left behind in order to pursue her dreams and a best friend she'd had a falling out with.

Natalie sounded like a simple person and a complicated one at the same time—simple in that she had a single goal, and she had gone out into the world to pursue it, not letting anybody or any circumstance get in her way.

Yet she was complicated because nobody seemed to know who she was. To some, she was sweet and hardworking. To others, she was mean spirited and a tyrant. Clémence supposed people all had these different facets. People in the city were so hardened sometimes, so cynical and jaded, like Tata, the makeup artist. She wished she could say these people were anomalies, but they seemed to be everywhere.

When the waiter came with her drink, her phone rang. It was Alice, Gabrielle's agent.

"Clémence, she's in. Gabrielle loves the idea."

"Really?" Clémence exclaimed, breathing a sigh of relief.

"Like I said, her schedule is packed, but she is willing to meet you. She has a shoot all day for a mascara tomorrow for BISOUX. You can drop in around lunch, at noon, and she'll have a quick chat with you. How's that?"

"Sounds great," Clémence said.

"Text me your email, and I'll forward you all the details about the shoot."

"I'll do that right now."

"Oh, and Clémence?"

"Yes?"

"I hear that you're an artist."

Clémence paused. "*Oui*. How did you know that?"

"I did a little research. Heard through the grapevine that you'll be having an art show."

"Yes, I am."

"Fashion and art can go hand in hand," Alice said. "I'm looking forward to seeing your art, but if you ever need to do publicity, my agency can help you. Just keep that in mind."

"Er, thanks."

When Clémence got off the phone, she was a little dumbfounded. She'd been getting more and more offers to be in the public eye recently, and she didn't completely understand it. Sure, she was an heiress and had a couple of socialite friends, but she had no modelling or acting talents, her style was just like the style of every other Parisian woman living in the 16th, 6th, or 7th arrondissement, and she didn't really want to be more famous.

Sometimes it felt like people were trying to cash in on her recent run-ins with the press. She'd hated her experience with the paparazzi. Yet perhaps Alice was right. If she wanted to make it as an artist—and not just show in her own salon de thé forever—she might have to start doing more publicity.

Fame could be a platform for good, but in her experience, it seemed to be used for evil more often than not.

Chapter 14

Clémence woke up to Rolling Stones songs in the kitchen. It must've been Arthur cranking up the music.

When she came out of the bathroom, Miffy was jumping at her feet, and Clémence followed her down the hall and into the kitchen.

Arthur was dancing. Horribly. She loved him very much, but the man didn't know what to do with his limbs when it came to music.

"What's going on?" Clémence laughed.

At the sight of her, he ran to her and picked her up, twirling her around.

"I got a promotion!" he said. "A bigger office, less work, and more of telling other people what to do. I'm now a project manager."

Arthur was a business consultant at a big firm.

"That's great!" Clémence exclaimed. "I didn't know you were up for a promotion."

"I didn't want to jinx it. I figured that if I didn't get it, I wouldn't be as disappointed."

Clémence grinned. "But you did get it."

"I just got the call this morning. Did I wake you up? It's not that early, is it?"

"No, I needed to wake up to prep for this Gabrielle meeting anyway," Clémence said. "You might've woken some neighbors though."

Arthur turned down the radio knob.

"You know, Clémence, I know your parents are coming back soon, and I should probably move out."

"Well, you won't be far. You have a room on the top floor."

"I know, but that place is a closet. I know my family is down on the third floor, but it's about time I bought my own place. Now that I'm able to, I can invest in an apartment. What do you think? Move in with me?"

Clémence was speechless. It was a lot to digest so early in the morning, but her natural inclination was, "*Oui!*"

Arthur beamed. "Great. We can start visiting apartments this week."

"But where? In the same neighborhood or a different one?"

"I don't know. Do you think you'd want to stay here because your store is here?"

"The 16th is great, but sometimes I feel like it's..."

"A bit too stuffy?" Arthur said.

"Yes. But I'm not sure if I want to move to a trendy neighborhood, either. We're not exactly party animals, either."

Arthur smiled. He looked so sweet when he did; Clémence had to pinch him on the cheeks.

"We're a young but boring old couple," Arthur said.

"Basically," Clémence agreed.

"Want some breakfast?" Arthur asked.

"Sure, what are you having?"

"Slices of salmon in a baguette."

"I'll have that with some Brillat-Savarin cheese."

"Coming right up."

Clémence giggled. She liked it when Arthur pretended to be a cook and a waiter in the kitchen; it was a game they played. He wasn't much of a cook, but he could make simple things. It was an improvement on how he had been brought up. He'd been raised by nannies and private chefs who catered to his every whim. Since he'd moved in with Clémence, at least he'd learned how to do his laundry, which, shockingly enough, he had not done all his adult life. Even when he had done a semester abroad, he had sent out his laundry.

Sometimes Clémence couldn't believe she was dating the same person, since he'd changed so much since she had met him. Arthur used to be a playboy and a spoiled rich boy, but after they started going out, more and more of his sweet side was revealed to her. Underneath all that bad boy nonchalance, Arthur was a man who had been waiting to be in a relationship with the right woman.

They'd both been able to heal and grow since they had gotten together. Clémence was slowly healing from her mistrust of men, finally allowing someone into her life again after her cruel breakup with her ex. Arthur was taking on the responsibilities that he had eschewed as a young man. He seemed ready to take the next step in investing in real estate.

Did that mean that he was ready for marriage as well?

Clémence brushed those thoughts away. She didn't want to think about marriage right now. That was too scary. It seemed like only yesterday that she'd become Arthur's girlfriend, and that was unbelievable in its own right. But to be somebody's wife? There was a note of finality to that. She believed in marriage, but marriage was forever. To think about it, to consider being in one, was a lot to take in.

After Arthur left for work, she got dressed. She wanted to be as inconspicuous as possible, so she dressed in a navy cashmere sweater and black cigarette pants. Wearing her signature black ballet flats and barely there makeup, she was ready to go. Her bob was growing out. It was probably time for another trim.

She was one of those people who had the same haircut all the time. Her black hair brought out the blue sparkle of her eyes. On special occasions, she wore eyeliner to make them pop even more, but just a smidgen of mascara was enough for this outing.

Clémence had never been on a commercial photo shoot before. It was taking place in a studio just outside Paris. She had to flag down a cab to go there.

The taxi took about twenty minutes to get to the studio. The driver listened to classical music the entire time. It put Clémence in a more relaxed mood.

He dropped her off before a square, industrial building in the middle of nowhere. The taxi drove away.

She was east of Paris, but she felt like she was far removed from the city now. It felt like she was standing in Brooklyn or Pittsburgh. She approached the door and knocked. No one answered.

Clémence waited a while and then knocked again.

Suddenly, the door opened, and the annoyed face of a surly-looking man in his late thirties poked out.

"Were you the one knocking?"

"Er, yes," Clémence asked.

"We were rolling. You could've ruined a take."

"Oh, I'm sorry. Did I?"

"No." He eyed her suspiciously. "But you could've. What are you here for? Background extra?"

"No. I'm actually here because I have an appointment to speak to Gabrielle. Maybe her agent Alice told you?"

"I don't know," he said briskly. "I'll have to check with my colleague. What's your name?"

She told him, and he disappeared to search for the colleague. The set they were filming in was obstructed by screens, so Clémence couldn't see what was going on. There were a lot of people coming and going, however, so they must've been between takes.

"This is Clémence?" A woman came to scrutinize her. She had on a headset and a clipboard.

"Yes. Hi." Clémence put on her most winning smile.

"Gabrielle's about to take a break soon. Why don't you wait by her chair, there."

"Oh, okay."

The woman pointed to a director's chair with Gabrielle's name on the back. The other chair also had a name on it, presumably the director's, so Clémence figured she should stand.

As Clémence walked toward the chair, Gabrielle came from the other direction, out of the sectioned set. She was wearing silver, and her hair was dyed a white blond with eyebrows to match.

Clémence thought she looked absolutely incredible. As Gabrielle walked closer, Clémence noticed how full her lashes were. They certainly sold the product.

When Gabrielle saw her, she broke into a warm smile, which took Clémence by surprise.

"You must be Clémence Damour," Gabrielle said.

"Yes, hello." Clémence received kisses on the cheeks.

Gabrielle frowned when she realized that Clémence would be standing.

"*Excusez-moi*, Gerard?" she called out.

A harried young man of about twenty-five stopped and seemed to want to melt at the sound of Gabrielle's voice. He looked alarmed at the fact that Gabrielle was actually talking to him.

"*Oui?*" he said dreamily.

"Can you please bring my friend a chair, too?"

"Of course. Right away." He smiled and scurried away. A moment later, Clémence was sitting beside Gabrielle in a chair.

"When Alice told me about the idea, I was so excited," Gabrielle said, her dark-blue eyes all lit up. It could be the flattering lights of the studio, the makeup, or just her overall beauty, but Clémence felt hypnotized by her. And her voice was warm like honey—or a honey trap.

"I'm glad," Clémence said.

"I love Damour, which is why I'm excited to meet you. My fiancé and I go to Damour every week to buy a box of macarons. We split it, but we usually end up fighting for them."

"Why don't you each buy your own box?"

"What's the fun in that?" Gabrielle laughed. "When you had the Marcus Savin collection, we bought all the flavors, too. I loved the opera cake macaron. You know, as a model, I can't eat too many sweets. Otherwise, I'd eat the whole store."

"You're telling me." Clémence was starting to relax in her presence. "That's what I do when I go in to work. So, about the collection. I'm thinking of doing four macaron flavors, and you can create them. I wanted to talk to you to get a sense of who you are. Alice suggested that since you're getting married, we can do a wedding-themed collection."

"Oh no," Gabrielle moaned. "That sounds cheesy."

"Really? I thought so, too, but it's true that it would sell."

"No. I want to do something more authentic."

"Great. Tell me about yourself. What are you interested in? Who are you? We know you from your glamorous image as a model, but what are you passionate about?"

"Those are good questions." Gabrielle bit her lips. "You know, I've been modelling since I was seventeen or eighteen. That's more than a decade now. I'm not usually very candid in interviews. I'm guarded and don't feel the need to expose myself. I've been going to a therapist lately, and I suppose I do that to protect myself. The thing is, my life, sometimes it feels too good to be true. I say this to you because you don't seem the type to be jealous. I can tell because you have a charmed life, too."

Clémence nodded. She did. She had a lot to be thankful for. She didn't have to worry about money. Her boyfriend was kind to her, and she had great friends. Her only worry was these pesky murders and trying to solve them.

She observed Gabrielle. It couldn't be true that she had done it, could she? Even as a woman, Clémence was falling under Gabrielle's spell. She could see now why Cyril was quick to dismiss the possibility that Gabrielle was a murderer. She was simply too charming and beautiful in real life.

"My life is good," Clémence confirmed.

"And you're not a journalist, so I can be candid with you," Gabrielle said. "There are not a lot of people, aside from my fiancé, who I can be candid with."

"Why is that? What about friends?"

She shook her head sadly. "I used to have friends. Until high school. Other girls seemed to turn on me, or they used my biggest weakness against me."

"What weakness?" Clémence said.

There was a look of shame in her eyes, but she took a deep breath. "I was dyslexic for a long time. As I child, I had a hard time learning how to read. I tried to keep it a secret by memorizing things. But once, in high school, I got called on in class to read a passage from a book. I did it, and the others found out." She shook her head, remembering the shame. "It was very humiliating. The other girls already resented me because of the way I looked, the way their boyfriends looked at me, and they started bullying me, calling me dumb. Even the boys did it. For that reason, I didn't go to college. That was around the time my modelling career took off anyway."

"That's sad," Clémence said.

"So my life now, with a man who worships me, despite knowing my faults, and working with the top people in the industry, I'm very lucky. I've come a long way in overcoming my dyslexia and the shame I used to feel. But I still have a problem opening up to people about that disability. That's why I still don't get too close to other women. Anyway, you're actually the first person outside of my family that I've revealed this to. I just don't want people thinking I'm dumb, you know? That the only thing I've got going for me is my looks."

"No, of course not."

"The world judges by appearances, and I've suffered by that but also made millions by it."

"We should make the macaron line about empowerment," Clémence said.

Gabrielle smiled. "I like it. And I'd like to donate my proceeds to an antibullying campaign I'm starting."

"Really? That's great."

"It's out of my comfort zone to be sharing my experiences about my past, but I think it'll help people."

"Well, if they see a supermodel has been bullied, it would definitely help."

Gabrielle breathed a sigh of relief. "I'm so glad. I've been thinking about this antibullying campaign for a long time, and who knew that macarons would be my opportunity to launch this platform."

Clémence felt tempted to become Gabrielle's best friend. There was something about her that was magnetic. Yet Clémence had to remind herself that Gabrielle was still a murder suspect.

Why did Clémence think she was guilty again?

"I saw you backstage at the Marcus Savin show," Clémence said. "But we didn't get a chance to meet."

"Oh, you were there?" Gabrielle said. "Fashion weeks are usually so hectic for me. I walk shows, yet I have photo shoots and commercial shoots at the same time. It was crazy, so I'm sorry we didn't get to meet."

"That's okay. I didn't have the chance to meet a lot of people, since it was a crime scene."

"Right," Gabrielle said sadly. "Poor girl. I didn't know what had happened at the time. I was so absorbed in trying to make my next appointment that I just went. If I had known, I would've stayed and cooperated, told what I know."

"What did you know?"

"Not a whole lot." She shook her head. "After the show, I went to the bathroom to change and then came back out. I don't like undressing backstage like the other girls, because photographers would sell my nude photos. They've done it before. I might've passed the room where she was killed, but I didn't see anyone in that hall."

"Why was Natalie so hated?"

"I didn't know she was hated," Gabrielle said. "She was a little gruff, but not to me."

"It's probably because you're a top model. Who else was she mean to?"

"Well..." Gabrielle thought about it. "I don't talk to a lot of people backstage. I'm ashamed to say this, but I don't like to socialize with the other models, because I had some bad experiences living in model apartments when I was younger. Some of the girls can be, well, catty to say the least, and it reminded me of my high school experiences. Backstage, I usually stick to talking to people I know."

That makes sense, Clémence thought. No wonder she was antisocial.

"I spent a lot of time talking to Tata. Do you know her?"

"Yes. I met her."

"She mentioned something about Natalie at some point. I can't remember what. I heard them debating about something earlier in the day. Something about animal rights. Natalie seemed passionate about something." Gabrielle thought about it for a moment. "Oh, I remember now. Tata was defending her makeup line. Her company tested on animals, and Natalie was a vegan. So Tata was very defensive, saying how sometimes you needed to harm a rabbit so humans wouldn't be harmed."

"Are you friends with Tata?"

"Friends? Well, I like working together. We're not close friends, but I do have a great working relationship with her."

"Do you by any chance think that Tata could be capable of killing a person?"

Chapter 15

Clémence sat on a stool in a corner of the Damour kitchen. Sebastien and Berenice were baking while Celine came in on her break to chat.

"What's new, Clémence?" Celine asked. "I feel like I haven't seen you in so long."

"I know. I've been busy. I'm waiting for this photographer to call me back."

"What photographer? Is this related to the case you're working on?"

Clémence nodded, still deep in thought. She snapped out of it when she realized she wasn't giving her friend enough attention.

"What's new with you?" she asked Celine.

"Oh, nothing," she said coyly. "Except when I was going to work today, a cute guy asked me to go to coffee."

"Did you?"

"Well, I didn't have time, but he asked for my number and I gave it to him. I'll be playing hard to get this time."

"That's going to be a challenge," Sebastien quipped.

"You shush," Celine said.

Clémence's cell phone rang. It was the photographer Clémence had left a message for. She picked up and began talking.

"...Yes. Please send me whatever photos you have...even if you have hundreds, that's fine. I'll look through them all. This is my email..."

After Clémence spelled out her email address, she thanked the guy and hung up.

"What was that about?" Berenice asked.

"New angle on the case," Clémence said. "It's not Gabrielle the supermodel."

"I knew it wouldn't be," Sebastien said. "She's too pretty, and kind of dumb."

Clémence glared at him. "She's not dumb. Plus, we just hired her for our next campaign, so you will actually be working with her. Take care not to say things like that to her to her face."

"Oh, there's an actual campaign now?" Sebastien said. "Okay, okay, I'm sorry. One minute she's the killer, the next minute she's not. I can't keep up with you."

"I think it's Tata, the makeup artist. Now, I don't know what shoes she'd been wearing; I wasn't paying attention at the time. What if she'd been wearing Styra shoes all along? I checked with the police, and they didn't check her shoes. Tata had left before that happened. I dismissed her because I'd already talked to her. I can't believe I forgot that we didn't check her shoes, and no one had mentioned that she was gone! There were just so many people backstage."

"Those fashion people probably get really distracted easily," Berenice said. "They're also probably pretty self-absorbed."

"It'll be too bad if Tata's the killer," Celine said. "I like her lip glosses. They stay on really well."

"Thanks to animal testing," Clémence muttered.

"What?"

"Nothing. Oh, the photographer just sent the photographs. He was a member of the press who had been taking photos of the show, then followed a journalist colleague backstage to interview Marcus. He did take some photos backstage, but he respected Marcus's instructions not to take photos of models in a state of undress."

Clémence glanced through the thumbnails of photos, searching for the ones backstage. She opened one picture of Tata taking off Gabrielle's makeup. She enlarged it on her iPad.

Clémence squinted. The photograph wasn't the clearest due to the dimmer lighting backstage.

"What are you looking for?" Sebastien asked.

Sebastien, Berenice, and Celine all came around to look at the photo on her iPad. Tata was wearing brown boots that came up to her knees.

"These boots," she replied. "Are these Styra shoes? I can't tell. Girls?"

Berenice and Celine both looked at each other. Berenice shrugged.

"I'm not a shoe expert, to tell you the truth," Berenice said.

"I hadn't even heard of the brand before you told me about it," Celine said.

"Don't look at me," Sebastien said, even though nobody was looking at him.

"I don't recall seeing these on the Styra website," Clémence muttered.

"Do another search," Berenice suggested. "Search 'Styra brown boots' and see what you come up with."

"That seems to be the only option." Clémence did just that. She scrolled through Google images until she was nearly at the bottom of the page. "Is that it?" She exclaimed when she saw a style similar to Tata's boots.

It took her to a personal blog written in English.

"These are from 2009," Clémence said. "From Styra's first season. These boots are old. Look, it says that they were only made in small batches, since the company was so new at the time. This is it. This is the proof I need."

"Why do you think Tata did it?" Celine said.

"When I talked to her, I got the impression that she was a sociopath—she knew someone had been killed, but she didn't seem to care. Now I hear that she'd had an argument with Natalie before she was killed and that she disappeared in the middle of the police investigation. Plus, now with the boots as proof, it has to be her."

"Oh no," Celine said. "This sucks, because now I won't feel right using her lip glosses, and I'll have to toss them."

Chapter 16

"I can't believe I let you talk me out of a busy day at the office to do this," Cyril groaned.

"Let's be honest," Clémence said. "You don't do much at that office. All you do is shuffle paper around a desk."

Cyril opened his mouth to protest, but Arthur cut in.

"Let's all be civil," Arthur said. "You're both here for a common goal."

Arthur had taken half a day off work to be by Clémence's side for moral support. In this case, he had to act as a mediator. Cyril and Clémence fought like cats and dogs, and they were both competitive.

"I still think Karmen is the culprit," Cyril said.

"What other proof do you need?" Clémence said. "Tata also wore Styra boots. Natalie threatened to ruin her reputation. So Tata killed her."

"Are you sure of yourself?" Cyril said.

"Are we going to make a wager on this?"

"Clémence," Arthur cut in again. "This is not a game. Nobody's placing any bets. We're here for the truth, not to incriminate anyone, okay?"

They were in Place de la Concorde, an area with numerous luxury jewelry and watch stores. Tata was doing makeup on a shoot for a high-end watch campaign. It was being held on the second floor of one of the exclusive buildings, above the watch store itself.

Cyril buzzed from the front door. "Paris police. Detective Cyril St. Clair."

Clémence heard people talking through the intercom but couldn't make out what they were saying. Ultimately, someone buzzed them in.

The three of them squeezed into the tiny elevator. When they went in, they found themselves in a storefront that was exclusively for private clients. Clémence willed herself not to be distracted by the beautiful watches and jewelry.

"Tata Milan?" Cyril called.

Tata stood up. She'd been touching up the makeup of a brunette American supermodel whose face Clémence recognized but whose name she couldn't recall. There was a small crew of around ten people at the shoot, and they all turned to stare at the newcomers.

"Can we speak to you in private?" Clémence said. She noticed Tata was wearing the same boots. They looked like the Styra ones she'd seen on the blog.

"I'm working." Tata frowned. "What's this about?"

"Inspector Cyril St. Clair." He flashed his badge proudly, walking toward her with the inflated chest of a rooster. "It's a serious matter, so if you can come with us—"

"I don't think you understand how much these people are paying for my time," she said. "If you have something to say, say it here. I have nothing to hide."

"Okay. You're arrested for the murder of Natalie Albert."

Tata kept calm and continued working on the model, even though everyone else was staring. Their jaws dropped, and they started whispering among themselves.

"That's ridiculous," Tata scoffed. "I'm not the murderer. I thought you caught the murderer already."

"Those shoes," Clémence said confidently. "They're Styra."

Tata looked her in the eye and laughed. "They're not. I knew you didn't know anything about fashion. I have no idea why you were sitting front row at

Marcus Savin's show. These are handmade from a family-run Italian shoe store in Florence."

"But..." Clémence looked at the boots more closely. The buttons at the side didn't have the Styra "S" logo.

"Do you want to see the bottoms of the boots?" Tata said boredly. "Is this what I have to do to prove that I'm not the murderer?"

She sighed and stood up. Holding on to the back of the model's chair, she bent one of her legs back. Cyril and Clémence peered down at the sole of the boot.

Tata was right. These were not Styra boots.

"Are we done?" Tata said.

"But..." Clémence said. "You and Natalie were arguing."

"Natalie argued with everyone," Tata said. "That's how some people like to get attention in this industry. But just because we had one small debate, it doesn't mean that I stuck a knife through her back."

"But..." Clémence's face burned. She wasn't used to being so utterly wrong.

"Who do you even think you are?" Tata said. "You're an heiress to some patisserie chain who never worked a day in your life. What are you doing playing detective? You have too much free time.

But it's at the expense of others. This is humiliating for me. How dare you barge onto my set like this?"

"We're sorry," Arthur said, then whispered to Clémence, "Come on, let's go."

"You're finished, Clémence," Tata snarled. "You're not fit to work in fashion, and I'll never work with you. I'll tell everybody I know to blacklist you."

Clémence looked at all the disapproving faces turned her way. She turned to go. Her cheeks burned. Arthur put his arm around her.

How could she have been so wrong?

Even Cyril knew not to chastise her, knowing that she'd been humiliated enough.

"I'm sorry," Clémence whispered.

"It's okay," Arthur whispered back.

When they got back out on the street, Cyril cleared his throat. "I'll be going back to my office now, where there's real work to be done."

He turned abruptly and walked away.

Clémence was grateful that Cyril didn't gloat too much.

She had been such an idiot. Tata was right. Who *did* she think she was? She was no detective. She wasn't good at anything, really.

Chapter 17

At the Damour patisserie the next morning, Clémence willed herself to go to work again. She helped Sebastien make pumpkin-flavored macarons, but she was still burning from the embarrassment of the day before.

She'd accused an innocent woman of murder. Even if she was not the most likeable person, Tata had been innocent nonetheless. Clémence couldn't remember the last time that her ego had been this bruised. She had been so wrong. Maybe she'd gotten too sure of herself after all the cases she had helped solve in the past—she got too cocky.

Had she been turning into a Cyril? Self-important, pompous, and delusional?

In any case, this experience had brought her back down to earth.

Tata had threatened to blacklist her. While Clémence didn't care that much to be working in the fashion industry, she didn't like the thought of people hating her. Perhaps when Clémence's ego recovered, she would apologize to Tata.

During her break, she opened her iPad and browsed through a few articles. With a cup of coffee by her side and a pain au chocolat fresh from the oven, she tried to relax. She sat in Carolyn's office, which was empty, since Carolyn didn't come in until eleven a.m.

Clémence checked her email and found a new email from the photographer with the subject line "Marcus Savin show 2". It was another batch of photos. He must've sent the two emails, one after another, but she'd only looked through the first one.

She opened the second email and looked through the photos simply out of curiosity. Since Gabrielle and Tata were both innocent, it had to be Karmen.

Unless...who was that figure lurking in the background in one of the photos? Clémence didn't know she had even been backstage. The woman had said she'd not been there, but it was unmistakable that it was her.

Suddenly Clémence knew who the killer was. She sprang out of her seat, ready to make a call to Cyril despite her destroyed reputation as the better sleuth.

Clémence waited in the outdoor cafe in the gardens of the Tuileries. The sun was out that day, and plenty of people were enjoying the scenic surroundings of the gardens and the fountains. If one stood in the middle of the Tuileries, the Louvre could be seen on one side and the Luxor Obelisk the other.

She was wearing a stylish outfit—a black leather pencil skirt with a patterned dark-green silk button-down shirt. A fitted, distressed brown leather jacket was worn over it, and black Louboutin pumps graced her feet. She had to dress more like a fashionista than usual, since she was about to be photographed.

Lucie appeared, camera in hand.

"Hi, Clémence! So glad you agreed to this."

Clémence stood up, and Lucie greeted her with kisses on the cheeks.

"No problem," Clémence replied brightly. "I thought this would be fun."

"Let's take some pictures of you from different angles." Lucie took the sense cap off her camera.

She snapped away while Clémence smiled. Lucie was a good photographer. She took all the photos on her blog, so Clémence could trust that she'd look good.

Lucie photographed her having coffee, fake laughing, posing near the trees, playing with a dog that came nearby.

Too bad the photos would never make it onto her blog by the time Clémence was done with her.

When Lucie finished, she sat down with Clémence and ordered a cappuccino.

Lucie got out her pen and notebook and asked her some questions.

"Who are your style inspirations?"

"My mother," Clémence replied. "I have a question for you as well."

Lucie looked up from her notebook. "Sure. What?"

"Why did you kill Natalie?"

Lucie's good-humored expression faded. She was speechless.

"I can take a guess," Clémence said. "Natalie wouldn't let you go backstage. Being the social climber that you are, you went back anyway."

"What proof do you have?" Lucie said.

"Photos. From a photographer. You weren't as careful as you thought. Sure, there were no cameras backstage, but there is always someone taking photos. You should know, since you're always snapping away."

"Show me," Lucie said. "Show me the photo."

Clémence got out her iPad and showed her. Lucie grabbed it and tried to break the iPad in half on the table. Other patrons turned to look at her. Lucie turned red, but she kept her voice low.

"Now you don't have the photo."

"It's on the Internet," Clémence said. "I know you were back there."

"You and who else?" Lucie looked around suspiciously.

"The fact that Natalie rejected you from backstage shouldn't be the only reason. So why? Why did you do it?"

Lucie let out a strange, high-pitched laugh. "For the fun of it. Nobody cares about a fashion blogger, especially a second-tier one with little influence. I was never the prettiest or the most stylish or anything. I would never amount to anything. My mother told me that. So I showed her. I showed everyone. If I can't get backstage and be where all the beautiful people are, I'll kill whoever stands in my way. And Natalie. She was a nobody, too. I hate her. I hate nobodies. And you know who else I hate? The somebodies. That's why I was trying to get you to see that it was Gabrielle."

"How?"

"You're always snooping around. I thought you'd find some dirt on her. I'm surprised you didn't. Gabrielle must really be an angel. She must be the only one in this industry." She let out another laugh.

Clémence thought that Lucie must be insane. "You didn't think the murder through, did you? You did it out of passion, then you fled, but then you thought you could pin it on someone else. It was the wrong person, but someone did get pinned nonetheless. Why did you try to sway me?"

"I knew Karmen was innocent, but that seemed too easy. I thought I'd have some fun with you and the police with the Gabrielle business. When you pinned the blame on yet another wrong victim, I would've convinced you to let me write about it for my site."

"I never talk about my cases," Clémence said.

"I would've written something anyway."

"Is that how desperate you are for attention? What do you want, anyway?"

"What everyone wants: fame, fans, adoration." Lucie looked at Clémence. "What about you? You're a girl on the verge. You could be a somebody, yet you want to be in the shadows. Why? What's your plan?"

"What plan? I like my privacy. I don't know why you're so calm. You're going to be arrested for murder."

"No. I don't think so," Lucie said. "A photo is nothing. Karmen is still the guilty one. The police have way more against her. Mob connections?" She shook her head.

Clémence only smiled. She crossed her arms and calmly sat back in her chair. Cyril and two of his men approached their little table.

Lucie looked up, surprised. She whipped her head back to Clémence.

"I told you," Clémence said coolly. "You're arrested for murder."

Cyril slapped handcuffs on one of her wrists and then twisted her other arm back.

"Ow, you're hurting me!" Lucie exclaimed.

"I guess you're feeling a fraction of what Natalie felt when you stabbed her," Clémence said.

Chapter 18

Wearing a mint strapless maxi dress, Clémence stood in a corner of the Damour *salon de thé* on a Saturday evening. All the guests had arrived for her art show, and she was nervous.

On the surface, she was all smiles, working the room and making sure people were taken care of. However, she couldn't bear to witness what people thought of her art. Even if it was paintings of dessert.

"Hey, are you okay?" Arthur came over to her.

"Of course I am," Clémence chirped.

Arthur gave her a knowing look. "Don't worry. People love your work. Two have already sold. I put red stickers next to them."

"Really? Which ones?"

Arthur led her to the one of three flying chocolate éclairs and another one of a pain au chocolat on a plate with a fork and knife beside it.

"Who bought them? Separate buyers?"

"I don't know. Ben just told me they were sold."

Ben was in charge of the sales. He was an outgoing Englishman who was good at talking to people. When Clémence caught his eye, he winked at her and went back to talking to two guests.

All her friends were in the room, along with her industry connections and family friends of her parents. Gabrielle was also there with her fiancé. She seemed particularly taken with the macaron painting.

Someone she didn't expect came through the doors: Tata Milan.

"*Bonsoir*," Clémence went over to greet her.

"*Bonsoir* yourself," Tata replied in her usual cold manner.

"What brings you here?" Clémence asked.

"I heard about how you helped the police capture that fashion blogger. I was impressed."

"Thanks," Clémence said.

"I got your flowers and card," Tata said. "And I do feel bad about saying those things to you. I was angry because I'm not used to being accused of murder, but what I said wasn't exactly classy, either."

"I understand why you were mad. I felt horrible for accusing you and for thinking you were the murderer. It was wrong of me to jump to conclusions like that."

"Well, all that's behind us. Let's just wipe the slate clean. How's that?"

Clémence smiled. "That would be great."

People could really surprise her sometimes. The nice ones could turn out to be killers and the grouchy ones to be really sweet. She had to keep learning not to take people at face value. First impressions weren't worth much.

If she judged people by first impressions, she'd never have been with Arthur.

After the guests had left, her friends drunk and gone home, and the caterers packed up and gone, Clémence and Arthur were left alone. She could finally breathe a sigh of relief.

Half of her paintings had sold, and she would donate her profits to Gabrielle's antibullying charity.

When she and Arthur went outside and locked up, she fell into Arthur's arms, hugging him tightly.

It was past one a.m., and Paris had never been so quiet. Even the lights of the Eiffel Tower were off.

"I love you," she said. "Crazy week, but as long as I can see you every night, I'm happy."

Arthur smiled. He looked adorable under the moonlight.

"I feel the same," he said softly. "You know how I suggested moving in together?"

Clémence nodded.

He got down on one knee. "How about moving in together *engaged*?"

He took out a box from his suit pocket. Clémence gasped.

Arthur opened the box. It was the most beautiful diamond set in rose gold.

"Will you marry me?" Arthur said.

For a moment, she remained speechless. Then a smile spread across her tired face, the widest she'd probably ever smiled.

"Yes, of course I'll marry you!"

Recipe #1

Classic Opera Cake Recipe

Makes 16

Ingredients for almond cake:

- 6 large egg whites, room temperature
- 2 tbsp. granulated sugar
- 6 large eggs
- 2 cups ground blanched almonds
- 2 1/4 cup icing sugar, sifted
- 1/2 cup all-purpose flour
- 3 tbsp. butter, melted and cooled

For coffee syrup:

- 1/2 cup water

- 1/3 cup sugar

- 1 1/2 tbsp. instant espresso

For coffee buttercream:

- 2 tbsp. boiling water

- 2 tbsp. instant espresso

- 1 cup sugar

- 1 tsp. vanilla extract

- 3 tbsp. water

- 1 egg

- 1 egg yolk

- 14 tbsp. butter, room temperature

For dark chocolate ganache:

- 1/2 cups whole milk

- 1/4 cup heavy cream

- 8 ounces bittersweet chocolate, finely chopped

- 4 tbsp. butter, room temperature

For chocolate glaze:

- 5 ounces bittersweet chocolate, finely chopped

- 1/2 cup butter

Instructions for almond cake:

Preheat oven to 425°F. Line two 15 × 12-inch pans with parchment paper. Butter paper. Set aside.

Beat egg whites on high until foamy. Slowly put in the granulated sugar, until it is all incorporated. Beat meringue until glossy and it holds stiff peaks.

In a separate bowl, beat ground almonds, icing sugar, and whole eggs on medium until mixture is light and foamy. Stir flour into the almond batter.

Gently stir 1/4 of almond batter into whipped egg whites. Fold the remainder of the almond batter and the melted, cooled butter into the egg whites.

Divide batter between two pans. Bake for 5 minutes until surface springs back with a light touch.

Cover top of each cake with fresh parchment. Carefully turn cake over. Peel back old parchment from bottoms of cakes. Cover cakes with the parchment to prevent them from drying.

For coffee syrup:

Bring water, sugar, and instant espresso to a boil in a small saucepan over medium heat. Let cool for 5 minutes. Set aside to brush on cake later.

For the coffee buttercream:

Stir together boiling water and espresso powder. Set aside mixture.

In a medium saucepan, over medium heat, bring sugar, vanilla, and 3 tbsp. water to a boil. Cook until it reaches 255°F on a candy thermometer. Remove mixture from heat and allow it to cool slightly.

In a bowl, beat egg and egg yolk until fluffy. Pour in sugar syrup while beating. Then mix in the coffee mixture. Continue beating on medium-high speed. Add butter slowly until fully incorporated. The buttercream is ready when it is thick and fluffy.

For the ganache:

Bring milk and cream to a boil in a medium saucepan over medium heat. Remove pan and stir in chocolate, 2 minutes. Stir in butter. Continue stirring ganache for 90 seconds.

To assemble the cake:

Line a large baking sheet with parchment paper. Cut a 10 × 10-inch square out of each layer of cake. Place first square on the baking sheet. Brush cake with espresso syrup. Spread 3/4 of coffee buttercream over the cake.

Place the two spare rectangles of cake over buttercream. Brush the pieces with espresso syrup. Spread chocolate ganache over the cake in a smooth layer.

Place last layer of cake over ganache. Brush with espresso syrup, then spread a thin layer of coffee buttercream.

Chill cake in fridge for 1 hour before glazing.

To glaze the cake:

Boil butter, discarding solids. Melt chocolate in a double boiler and stir in butter until glaze is smooth.

Pour chocolate glaze over cake. Allow it to set in fridge before serving.

Recipe # 2

Green Tea Opera Cake Recipe

Ingredients for green tea cake:

- 3 large egg whites, room temperature
- 1 tbsp. granulated sugar
- 1 cup ground almonds
- 1 cup icing sugar, sifted
- 3 large eggs
- 1 tbsp matcha
- 1/4 cup all-purpose flour
- 1 1/2 tbsp. unsalted butter, melted and cooled

For syrup:

- 1/4 cup water
- 1 1/4 tbsp. granulated sugar
- 1 tsp. green tea liqueur

For green tea buttercream:

• 1/2 cup sugar

• 1 tbsp. matcha

• 2 large egg whites

• 3/4 cup unsalted butter, room temperature

For chocolate ganache:

• 7 oz. chocolate, chopped

• 1/2 cup + 2 tbsp. heavy cream

For chocolate glaze:

• 3 ounces chocolate, chopped

• 1/4 cup heavy cream

Instructions for cake:

Preheat oven to 425°F.

Line a 12.5 × 15.5-inch pan with parchment paper and then grease it with butter. Beat egg whites in a bowl until soft peaks form. Add granulated sugar. Beat until peaks are stiff and glossy.

In another bowl, beat almonds, icing sugar, matcha, and eggs until light and voluminous. Add flour and beat until flour is combined. Fold the meringue into the mixture.

Fold in the butter.

Pour the batter into the pan. Bake until lightly browned and springy to the touch, about 5 to 9 minutes.

Loosen cake in pan by running a knife along the edges. Cover cake with parchment paper. Flip over. Peel parchment paper off, but cover cake with it while it cools to prevent drying.

For syrup:

Bring all ingredients to a boil in a small saucepan. Stir until sugar is dissolved. Remove from heat and let cool.

For green tea buttercream:

Mix sugar and matcha in a small bowl. Whisk them into egg whites in a bowl over a pan of simmering water for about 3 minutes, until mixture is hot to the touch. The sugar should be dissolved.

Remove bowl from heat. Beat until cream is cool, about 5 minutes. Beat in butter one stick at a time. Beat the mixture until it thickens and becomes smooth, about 5 to 20 minutes.

For chocolate ganache:

Melt the chocolate in the heavy cream in a double boiler. Let cool for 10 minutes.

Assembling the cake:

Cut cake into four 6 × 7-inch pieces. Place 1 sheet of cake on a baking sheet. Moisten with syrup. Spread half of the buttercream over the cake.

Place 1 sheet of cake on top of the buttercream and moisten with syrup. Spread chocolate ganache on top of that cake.

Place 1 sheet of cake over the ganache. Moisten with syrup. Spread remaining buttercream over the cake.

Place 1 sheet of the cake on top of the buttercream. Moisten with syrup.

Pour the glaze over the cake and smooth it out. Refrigerate until it sets, about 30 minutes. Trim the sides for a smooth finish.

.

$\mathcal{R}$ecipe #3

Orange-Vanilla Opera Cake

Ingredients for vanilla cake:

- 2 tbsp. unsalted butter, melted and cooled

- 3 large egg whites, room temperature

- 1 tsp. granulated sugar

- 1 cup ground blanched almonds

- 1 cup icing sugar, sifted

- Pinch salt

- 1/2 teaspoon vanilla

- 1 vanilla bean, split and scraped

- 1/4 cup all-purpose flour

- 3 large eggs

For syrup:

- 1/4 cup water
- 1.2 oz. granulated sugar
- 1 tbsp. Grand Marnier liqueur

For buttercream:

- 1/4 cup granulated sugar
- 1 large egg white
- 6 tbsp. unsalted butter, room temperature
- 1 tbsp. fresh orange juice
- 1/4 tsp. pure vanilla extract

For white chocolate mousse:

- 3.5 oz. white chocolate
- 1/2 cup + 1 1/2 tbsp. heavy cream
- 1/2 tbsp. Grand Marnier liqueur

For orange glaze:

- 2 cups powdered sugar, sifted
- 2 tbsp. unsalted butter
- 2 oranges, juiced and zested

Instructions for cake:

Preheat the oven to 425 degrees. Line a 12.5 × 15.5-inch pan with parchment paper and brush with 1/2 tablespoon of the melted butter.

Whip egg whites on low speed until foamy. Then whip on medium-high speed until whites hold soft peaks. Add granulated sugar. Whip on high speed until the whites are stiff and glossy.

In a separate bowl, beat almonds, eggs, icing sugar, salt, and vanillas on medium speed until light and voluminous, about 3 minutes. Add flour and beat at low speed until it disappears.

Use rubber spatula to gently fold meringue into almond mixture. Then fold the remaining melted butter until combined. Spread batter evenly in the prepared pan.

Bake cake until slightly browned and springy to the touch, 5 to 9 minutes.

Run knife along edges of cake to loosen from pan. Cover pan with parchment paper and turn pan over. Carefully peel away the parchment, but use parchment to cover the cake to prevent from drying. Cool at room temperature.

For syrup:

Combine water and sugar in a small saucepan. Bring to a boil while stirring to dissolve ingredients.

Stir in liqueur. Remove from heat and allow syrup to cool.

For buttercream:

Mix sugar and egg white in a bowl over simmering water until bowl feels hot, about 3 minutes. The sugar should be dissolved. Remove bowl from heat.

Beat meringue on medium speed until cooled to room temperature, about 5 minutes.

Add the butter 2 tablespoons at a time. Once all the butter is in, beat buttercream on medium-high speed until it is thick and very smooth, about 6 to 10 minutes. If buttercream curdles or separates, keeping beating.

On medium speed, beat in orange juice, waiting until each addition is absorbed before adding more, then the vanilla. The buttercream should be smooth and velvety.

For white chocolate mousse:

Melt chopped white chocolate and 3 table-spoons of heavy cream. Whisk gently. Cool at room temperature.

Place heavy cream in a bowl and mix. Add liqueur. Beat on high speed until soft peaks form. Stir 1 cup of whipped cream into the cooled white chocolate mixture. Fold in the remaining cream.

Don't overmix. Cover and refrigerate until ready to use.

For orange glaze:

Combine all ingredients over a double boiler. Cook until sugar and butter are melted and mixture has thickened. Pour through a fine mesh strainer. Beat until smooth and slightly cool.

Assembling the cake:

Cut and trim cake into three 10 × 5-inch rectangles. Place 1 cake on a baking sheet lined with parchment and moisten gently with 1/3 of syrup. Spread half the buttercream over this layer.

Top with another piece of cake. Moisten with 1/3 of syrup. Spread the remaining buttercream on the cake and then top with third cake.

Use remaining syrup to wet the cake. Refrigerate until very firm, at least 30 minutes.

Spread the mousse on the top layer of cake. Refrigerate for 2 to 3 hours for the mousse to firm up.

Pour cooled glaze over the top of the chilled cake, spreading to evenly coat the cake if necessary. Refrigerate the cake again to set the glaze.

Serve slightly chilled.

About the Author

Harper Lin lives in Kingston, Ontario with her husband, daughter, and Pomeranian puppy. When she's not reading or writing cozy mysteries, she's in yoga class, hiking, or hanging out with her family and friends. *The Patisserie Mysteries* draws from Harper's own experiences of living in Paris in her twenties. She is currently working on more cozy mysteries in several different series.

www.HarperLin.com

20169747R00100

Made in the USA
Middletown, DE
17 May 2015